## "There's one thing I'm good at . . ."

Garrett reached for a towel as he murmured, "And I'd better concentrate on doing it well."

Katy closed her eyes, enjoying a deep, sensual pleasure that was still new to her as he caressed her slowly, drying her with the towel. He used the terry cloth to tease her nipples, then leaned down and kissed each with great care.

"Do you like that, Katy?" he whispered.

"Everything you do feels right," she replied, her voice husky with desire. Katy could hardly stand. She wrapped her arms around him. "Hold me," she pleaded.

"I'll hold you, Katy," he said gently as he carried her to the bedroom. "I'll hold you so tight and so close that you'll never want to leave."

**Jayne Ann Krentz** was inspired to write *Test of Time* by her long-standing love of horses. When she was twelve, a rodeo-circuit cowboy regularly let her ride his horse, Rusty. Like Red Dazzle in *Test of Time*, Rusty was a usually placid, slow-moving quarter horse, but in a rodeo he was explosive, a glorious performer with all the speed and style imaginable. The story of Katy and Garrett also attracted Jayne because she wanted to portray "a postwedding courtship."

A very successful and popular author, Jayne lives in Seattle with her husband and their bird, Ferd.

## Books by Jayne Ann Krentz

HARLEQUIN TEMPTATION
146–THE FAMILY WAY
157–THE MAIN ATTRACTION
168–CHANCE OF A LIFETIME

HARLEQUIN INTRIGUE
10–LEGACY
17–THE WAITING GAME

# Test of Time

## JAYNE ANN KRENTZ

# Harlequin Books

TORONTO • NEW YORK • LONDON
AMSTERDAM • PARIS • SYDNEY • HAMBURG
STOCKHOLM • ATHENS • TOKYO • MILAN

Published November 1987

ISBN 0-373-25277-3

Printed in Canada

# 1

THE BRIDE took another shaky sip of champagne and wondered for the thousandth time that day if she was making the biggest mistake of her life.

Katy Randall Coltrane tightened her grip around the glass in her hand in an effort to still the trembling fingers. If she wasn't careful she was going to spill the expensive champagne all over her beautiful gown. That would definitely be a shame, considering the time she had spent selecting the lovely confection of satin and silk.

*Bridal jitters*, she told herself forcefully. That's all this stupid anxiety amounted to—a bad case of bridal jitters. Surely all brides suffered from such assaults on the nerves. If wedding day jitters weren't a common problem, a label wouldn't have been coined to describe them. Everything was all right. Nothing had changed. There was no reason to develop a frightening sense of doubt at this late stage. All along she had been telling herself she knew what she was doing and that what she was doing was the right thing.

Everything would work out. After all, she was head over heels in love with the man who had just taken his vows alongside her. Furthermore, she was twenty-eight years old. Old enough to know what she was doing.

Of course, it hadn't helped her morale any to accidentally eavesdrop on that conversation taking place out in the hotel gardens a few minutes earlier. Served her right for not asking directions to the rest rooms, Katy told herself. If she had, she would never have taken the wrong turn that had brought her within ear-shot of two of her mother's acquaintances. The words still burned in her ears.

"The Randalls are certainly sending their one and only daughter off in a first-class manner," Leonora Bates had remarked. "This little bash must have cost Harry and Wilma a fortune."

"They can afford it," her companion had said easily. "If you ask me, they're probably thanking their lucky stars Katy found a husband, any husband at all. Katy's such a quiet, diffident little creature. I didn't think she was interested in anything except managing her father's horse-breeding programs. I wonder how her mother feels about her new son-in-law, though?"

"Wilma accepts Coltrane because her husband approves of him. She trusts Harry's judgment in people. And you know as well as I do that Harry Randall has a habit of judging people on their own merits, not on their background. And Katy didn't exactly find herself a husband," Leonora had said meaningfully. "He found her. In fact, if you want my opinion, Garrett Coltrane took one look at quiet little Katy Randall and decided she was just what he wanted. By marrying her, he marries into several generations' worth of respectability and good social connections. Not to mention money."

"Coltrane's obviously done well for himself financially in that farm-and-ranch-management consulting business of his," the other woman had pointed out. "He's got money now."

"True," Leonora had agreed, "but in his own mind that probably doesn't make up for his dirt-poor background, his lack of a classy education and his wild reputation. The man's an ex-rodeo hand, for heaven's sake. Marrying Katy Randall will go a long way toward making people forget just how rough his past is."

"You know, when that boy left town to join the rodeo, I thought we'd all seen the last of him. Who would have thought he'd come back after all these years and marry the daughter of the man who used to employ him to clean out stables?"

"I wonder if sweet little Katy knows what she's getting into."

"It makes you think, doesn't it?"

Leonora had chuckled. "I'll say it does. It makes me think that Garrett Coltrane is one hard, ruthless, shrewd sonova..."

Katy had slipped away before Leonora had finished voicing her opinion of Garrett Coltrane.

Now, sheltered behind a row of leafy plants in the hotel's elegant reception room, Katy nervously glanced down at the band of gold on her left hand. The ancient symbol of her new marriage flashed warmly in the lights of the ballroom chandeliers. She was thinking how very primitive the ring looked, when a laughing voice sliced into her reverie.

"So this is where the new bride is hiding out. What do you think you're doing sneaking around over here behind the potted palms, Katy? This is your day. You're supposed to be the center of attention. You should be out there in the crowd, mingling."

Katy's head snapped up in startled surprise, and she swung around abruptly, the long, heavy skirts of her full gown swirling about her ankles. "Oh, hello, Julie. I wasn't hiding out, I was just—" She broke off as her weak ankle started to give way beneath the combined forces of her sudden off-balance movement and the heavy, swinging weight of her gown.

Automatically she put out a hand to steady herself and succeeded in grabbing the rim of a huge clay pot that held a monstrous fern. Long green fronds bobbed lazily, caressing her face, and champagne spilled from Katy's glass into the rich loam that filled the pot.

"Damn," Katy muttered, righting herself quickly and simultaneously spitting a bit of fern out of her mouth.

"What a way for a bride to talk on her wedding day." Julie Talbot reached out to put a steadying hand under Katy's elbow. "Are you okay?"

"Of course. I'm fine. It's just my ankle. I took it by surprise, and it doesn't handle surprises well. You know that."

Julie grinned with the ease of an old friend. Fair-haired and blue-eyed, Julie was an attractive woman the same age as Katy. A year before, Julie had married the scion of one of the well-to-do families who lived in the local community.

That community, which Katy had called home all her life, was a small enclave of wealthy, established Californians who inhabited a prestigious section of the Southern California Gold Coast. There were wealthier towns in the state but few that boasted as much pedigreed social assurance. The residents of the small, charming, expensively quaint town considered themselves a cut above the glitzy, tacky Los Angeles crowd up the coast, most of whom had made their fortunes in films and limited partnership deals.

The members of the Randalls' social circle enjoyed the self-confidence and refinement that comes from knowing one's money and land can be traced back further than one generation. Some of the locals could trace their heritage all the way back to Spanish land-grant days. In California, that constituted an impressive heritage.

The Randalls' friends did not get involved in films or limited partnerships. They invested in land and fabulously expensive horses and pre-Columbian artifacts. Many enjoyed playing gentleman farmer. They were shrewd business people who managed their inherited capital with great care.

Such people usually hired folks from Garrett Coltrane's side of the tracks to work their land, look after their horses and tend their beautiful gardens. It wasn't often that someone from the working class segment of the community married into Katy's socioeconomic class. Katy was well aware that Leonora Bates probably wasn't the only one commenting on Garrett's coup. She told herself it didn't matter. She and Garrett were in love, and she sensed instinctively that Garrett was far too proud to marry for money.

"I wasn't sure if it was the ankle or too much champagne," Julie said. "For your ankle's sake, though, I'm glad you had the sense to stick to flat shoes this afternoon. I was afraid you'd try to wear a pair of high heels down the aisle."

Katy made a very unbridelike face. "I'm not that idiotic. If I had tried to wear heels, I would have ended up in a heap at Garrett's feet. Very embarrassing."

"For you, not for Garrett. I think it would take a lot more than his bride falling at his feet in the middle of

the wedding service to shake your new husband." Julie
sent a thoughtful glance across the room to where Garrett Coltrane was deep in conversation with a small
group of male wedding guests.

Garrett wasn't doing much of the talking. As usual,
he listened in calm, thoughtful silence while others
spoke. But when he finally said something, everyone
else in the group would stop and listen. Coltrane had
that effect on those around him, regardless of his lis-
teners' financial or social status. It was an inborn talent and one he had apparently used in recent years to
help establish his successful consulting firm. He was the
kind of man to whom other people automatically paid
attention.

Katy followed her friend's gaze, chewing off what
remained of her peach-colored lipstick as she studied
her new husband with anxious eyes. Julie was right. It
would take a lot to shake Garrett's granite-tough self-
assurance. He was a man who knew what he wanted,
where he was going and how he was going to get there.
He was fortified for the tasks he set himself with a vast
reservoir of strength that was both physical and emotional.

He was not a tall man; probably a notch or two under six feet in height, which made him slightly shorter
than Katy's father. But when he stood in a group, he
was the man you noticed first.

There was a supple leanness about him, a smooth,
coordinated sense of animal grace that was even more
evident when he was in a saddle. There was obvious
power in his shoulders and thighs but no dramatic bulge
of muscle.

Coltrane's hair was charcoal dark. He wore it short, and when he was outdoors it was usually covered with an expensive Stetson. Coltrane's features were bluntly hewn, and he had a forceful jawline. There was nothing delicate or soft about him, but there was, Katy had decided, something very intriguing about his eyes. They were an unusual shade of amber, a warm, golden color that Katy hoped would one day reflect the feelings she felt certain he had for her.

Garrett Coltrane was from an old-fashioned breed of male. The kind of man who was destined to make his own way in life and do it on his own terms. *The strong, silent type*, Katy had told herself time and again. If he were a stallion she would put him into a breeding program in spite of his lack of elegant good looks. She would want to capture his strength, endurance and determination. Such qualities should not be lost in either horses or humans.

Garrett had no talent or inclination to discuss his own emotions, but Katy had been sure all along that he was capable of great depth of feeling. Just because he could not or would not talk about his feelings did not mean he was unemotional. Katy had been sure of her analysis, sure that deep down Garrett loved her in his own strong, silent way.

At least she had been sure when she had accepted his calm, unemotional offer of marriage.

Katy wasn't certain just when during the four weeks since she had accepted Garrett's offer of marriage she had begun to question his real feelings for her. She had pushed the gathering cloud of uncertainties firmly to the back of her mind while she busied herself with the myriad tasks of planning a wedding and the move to Garrett's home.

The soft, hidden, romantic streak in her nature had led Katy into organizing a magnificent wedding. She had wanted everything to be perfect. Her mother had been delighted to help, and together they had produced a beautiful ceremony and reception. Everyone in the community had been invited, and everyone had accepted the invitation. The whole affair had gone off like clockwork.

But today as she had walked carefully down the aisle to join Coltrane at the altar, the storm of doubts and fears had begun to break free inside Katy's mind.

"Bridal jitters," Julie said easily beside her. "Relax."

Katy's mouth curved ruefully. She should have known Julie was bound to detect the attack of nerves. "Did you have them?"

"A small dose," Julie admitted. "Don't worry about it. You'll get over them. Let's see your ring."

Katy obediently held out her hand to allow Julie to examine the plain gold band. "Garrett is the old-fashioned type. He isn't very interested in fancy jewelry."

"Hmm. I see what you mean. But I like it, Katy. There's something fitting about it. It looks right on you, if you know what I mean."

"A plain ring for a plain woman?"

"Don't be silly. You always look attractive, and today you look downright beautiful. You were glowing as you came down the aisle."

"I think that was sweat."

"What on earth are you talking about?"

Katy grinned briefly. "All right—a fine, delicate sheen of perspiration. Does that sound better? That was probably what was causing the glow you think you saw. I was scared to death."

Julie giggled. "Well, you looked terrific. I like your hair down around your shoulders like that." She eyed Katy's dark ash-brown hair with a critical eye. "It looks good down. You should wear it that way more often."

"Maybe," Katy replied noncommittally. Garrett had said nothing about her hair today. Of course, he had never said anything about her usual style—a neat, businesslike twist—either. Garrett wasn't the kind of man who paid much attention to a woman's clothing or her hairstyle.

"Back to this ring," Julie went on determinedly, "I think it's a very appropriate sort of wedding ring." Her blue eyes twinkled. "Did you know that wedding rings are ancient symbols of fertility?"

Katy grimaced. "Trust a horse person to remember that bit of lore."

"Horse people worry a lot about fertility. You of all people should know that. Your family has been breeding those beautiful Arabians since before you were born, and you've been managing the Randall breeding program for the past four years. Very successfully, too, I might add. Makes one wonder if maybe you used your knowledge of breeding selection to pick your husband."

"Julie! For heaven's sake. What a thing to say."

Julie laughed delightedly, drawing the attention of some of the guests who happened to be standing within hearing distance on the other side of the ferns. They smiled as they spotted the bride talking privately to her friend.

"Frankly, I think Garrett will make an excellent stud," Julie went on, undaunted. "Viewed in strictly technical terms, the two of you should make a perfect match. You've got the aristocratic bloodlines and he's got strength and stamina. I can't wait to see the kids. Neither can your parents, if you ask me."

Katy blushed a vivid pink as her friend put into words the very thoughts Katy herself had been thinking. "I'm sure my parents haven't even begun to think about grandchildren."

"That's what you think. Your parents can't wait for a grandchild. It's my guess they'll be counting nine months from the wedding night and marking their calendar."

Katy's mouth tightened, and the brief sense of amusement she had been experiencing faded. "They had better not be holding their breath. I have no intention of being rushed into anything as important as having a baby."

"What about Garrett?" Julie demanded. "Doesn't he have a say in the matter?"

"Garrett and I haven't discussed children," Katy admitted quietly. If the truth were known, it was one of many personal topics they had not yet discussed.

Julie frowned. "No offense, but wouldn't it have been smart to talk about something that basic before you two made wedding plans?"

Katy felt her flush intensify. She glanced away from her friend. "Garrett is a very private person. It isn't always easy to talk to him about...about certain things."

"And you suffer from the same kind of reserve," Julie accused. "Makes me wonder what the two of you do talk about when you're together. But, Katy, you can't be shy about discussing things like children. Good grief, this is your future that's at stake."

"Don't worry about it, Julie. I know what I'm doing."

Julie's eyes narrowed thoughtfully. "I thought you did, but for some reason I'm suddenly not so sure."

"Thanks a lot. I'm twenty-eight years old, I'm considered intelligent and I've had a good education. I'm marrying a man with whom I have business and professional interests in common. It's a very logical thing for me to be marrying Garrett Coltrane. It makes perfect sense. Give me a little credit."

"I don't know." Julie was still obviously doubtful. "You're a woman in love. That wipes out a lot of the benefits of intelligence and education and logic."

Katy groaned at Julie's insight. So much for keeping her own feelings hidden. "Some friend you are."

"Well, I'll take comfort in the knowledge that even if you don't know what you're doing, Garrett probably does."

"He always seems to, doesn't he?" Katy agreed with an uneasy feeling. She covered the prickle of uncertainty with her best smile as her beaming mother came through the crowd in search of her daughter.

On the other side of the room Garrett glanced toward the cluster of huge potted ferns and saw Katy standing amid the greenery. She was talking to her mother and Julie Talbot. Garrett nodded to himself, satisfied that Katy had not managed to retreat to the sidelines at her own wedding.

She was quite capable of doing exactly that, he reflected. It wasn't that she was shy or inhibited. She was simply quiet and restrained. She didn't go around calling attention to herself. A very calm, quiet woman. Not the sort to hold center stage or go all dramatic in front of an audience. She had a sort of subdued, refined classiness. He liked that. It was one of the many small things he liked about Katy Randall.

No, he reminded himself with an unexpected feeling of possessiveness, she wasn't Katy Randall any longer. She was Katy Coltrane as of an hour ago.

There was something very satisfying about having everything in his life falling into place at last. He had a business that was expanding rapidly, a new home that suited the life-style he was carving out for himself, and now he had a wife who would function as both business partner, hostess and, well, as a *wife*.

A wife. His wife.

He now had a woman for his bed as well as an acknowledged expert on equine breeding programs for his high-powered consulting staff. He had someone to share breakfast with as well as someone with whom he could discuss business problems.

Until this past week he hadn't given more than casual thought to what having a wife was actually going to mean in personal, physical terms.

The decision to marry Katy had been almost instantaneous when he had seen her for the first time after all those years. He had paid a visit to the Randall Stud Farm because he knew it was one of the best managed in the state. It was true he was professionally interested in seeing that management firsthand. But a part of him acknowledged he had wanted to show Harry Randall that the wild kid Randall had given a job to when no one else would had eventually turned out all right.

It had been a surprise to learn that the little solemn-faced girl who had spent all her spare time hanging around her father's stables was now the brilliantly intuitive manager of the Randall breeding programs. Somehow it hadn't startled Garrett to learn that Katy had not turned into the sophisticated debutante type. Her whole world as a child had been filled with horses, and apparently nothing much had changed over the years except that she no longer rode.

On some gut level Garrett had known instantly that the grown-up version of Katy Randall would suit him perfectly as a wife. He had briefly tried to analyze his certainty and had come to the conclusion that it was all very simple. He had found himself an intelligent, sensible young woman who would fit right into his business and his life. She would be an asset to the consulting firm, and she would be comfortable with the kind of people he now saw socially.

Garrett was convinced Katy wasn't going to turn temperamental or difficult on him the way a more sophisticated woman might have. She would not grow bored and difficult when the novelty of being married faded. She was not the kind to wander off in search of adventure, amorous or otherwise. She had proved that, when she had come back to her father's stud farm after she had gotten her master's degree and tried working in Los Angeles. Instead of staying to make her future amid the bright lights of the city, she had come running back home and promptly settled down on her father's farm.

Garrett liked the way Katy seemed eager to please him, and he liked the fact that she could talk about the things that were important to him and to his business. She was also attractive in a quiet, refined way. There was no other man in the picture. All things considered, Garrett had seen no reason that he and Katy shouldn't get along very well together. Katy had plainly been of the same opinion.

But tonight was his wedding night and Garrett found himself thinking of other things besides the logical considerations that had led to his marriage. He had a right to enjoy this evening. After all, he had taken on the responsibilities of a husband today. There was a gold ring on his hand to prove it.

Garrett glanced down at the ring. He wouldn't wear it all the time, of course. It was dangerous for a man who worked outdoors a lot to wear rings. Even though he was now called a consultant, Garrett still spent a lot of time in stables, barns, pastures and farm fields. It was all too easy to lose a finger by having a ring catch on a stray nail or a sliver of metal. But he didn't mind wearing the ring for social occasions. And he liked the idea of Katy wearing hers all the time. It was a way of telling other men she was taken.

Garrett shifted slightly, aware of a deep anticipation that was purely physical in nature. His mouth curved ruefully in very private amusement. No doubt about it, he was beginning to think more and more about the rights and privileges he had gained along with his new status as a husband today.

Lifting the glass in his hand to sample the good champagne Harry and Wilma Randall had bought for the occasion, Garrett listened to the conversation going on around him while he surreptitiously studied his bride.

Calm, quiet, serene, gentle, intelligent, comfortable. Those were all adjectives that came to mind whenever he thought of Katy. She wasn't going to drive him crazy by demanding exotic vacations to far-off places or frequent trips to the bright lights of the city. In spite of her background, she was accustomed to a quiet life-style that revolved around the demands of the horse business. She would adapt easily to Garrett's life-style.

But it wasn't her adaptability Garrett was thinking about right then. Instead, he found himself wondering if Katy was going to lose any of that calm, quiet, gentle serenity in bed. He had speculated more than once during the past few weeks on what it would be like to go to bed with Katy. Judging from the gentle, almost shy manner in which she had responded to his kisses, he assumed she would be soft and sweet and very undemanding in bed. He sensed her experience was quite limited, and he told himself that should make things easy on him. She wouldn't be making a lot of awkward comparisons.

But he wanted to please her, Garrett realized. He wanted her to be happy and contented with her lot in life. Tonight he would do his best to bring her pleasure in bed.

He just hoped her natural restraint would not cause her to freeze up completely on him. He was not a Don Juan or a Casanova. He was thirty-five years old and he had known a few women in his life, but the truth was, he'd spent a lot more time with horses and cattle than with females of his own species.

The whole matter of mating was a lot simpler and easier for horses and cattle. They didn't have several thousand years of civilization to contend with, in addition to the basic instincts.

Garrett thought about that as he studied Katy. He tried to imagine her with her dark brown hair fanned out around her on a pillow. Her hair was very soft, he had discovered the first time he'd impulsively thrust his fingers into it.

The action had been unpremeditated. He had been standing beside Katy at a paddock fence, watching a new foal discover the wonders of the great outdoors in the company of its attentive mother when a brisk wind had arisen. Katy's neat hair had been blown into a tangled mane. She had laughingly clutched at it, but before she could control the dark stuff Garrett had caught a handful of it in his fist. He could still remember the silky feel of it between his fingers. He wondered now what her hair would feel like on the naked skin of his chest and thighs.

Tonight when she lay in bed beside him she would be looking up at him with those wide, serious gray eyes of hers. He imagined the feminine curiosity and, perhaps, the eagerness, that would be lighting those eyes and felt his body grow taut at the mental image. He liked Katy's eyes. They reflected honesty and warmth and intelligence. You could tell a lot about a mare by her eyes, Garrett told himself. There was no reason to think you couldn't tell a lot about a woman the same way.

Garrett found himself mentally stripping the full wedding gown from Katy's slender figure and trying to imagine what he would discover underneath the silk and satin. He had already seen enough of her in jeans and snug knit tops to have a fair idea of what to expect.

She was a few inches shorter than he was, somewhere in the vicinity of five feet, four inches. Her figure had a neat, compact quality to it. If she'd been an Arabian, he would have described her conformation as excellent. Small and delicate, but sound, like a well-built mare. Sound, that is, except for her left ankle.

Her breasts were high and gently curved, her waist small, her hips nicely flared. It was true her slight limp marred the sense of gracefulness that delineated the rest of her body, but Garrett found himself rarely noticing her slightly halting stride. When he did, he found it oddly endearing. It occurred to him that a bad ankle was not going to matter one bit in bed.

Not for the first time today he wondered why he hadn't made an effort to get Katy into bed before the wedding. Realistically speaking, part of the problem had been logistics. After his initial visit to the farm, he hadn't been able to manage a lot of time with Katy. The demands of his own business had kept him occupied at the home office in San Luis Obispo. The courtship of Katy Randall had been conducted in a series of short, hurried weekend visits. In addition to the timing problems, there had been the added complication that Katy lived within shouting distance of her parents. She had a small cottage near the main house, and Garrett wasn't honestly sure how she would feel if her parents knew he had spent the night with their one and only daughter, even if she was twenty-eight. He hadn't wanted to commit any unforgivable social blunders at that stage of the game.

In addition to the logistics of the situation, Garrett had told himself that Katy wasn't the kind of woman who should be rushed.

There had been a lot of good reasons for not rushing off to bed with Katy, Garrett decided. But he was honest enough to admit there had been one final, half-understood explanation for his hesitation.

The truth was that a part of him had worried that Katy might change her mind about marrying him if he didn't perform up to her expectations in bed. The problem was that Garrett hadn't known for certain what sort of expectations a gently bred, possibly inhibited young woman of Katy's background would hold. He had been half afraid of lousing up his chances of marrying her by lousing up the seduction. It was very much out of character for him to have such qualms. Garrett had learned long ago to go after what he wanted and not allow uncertainties or doubts to get in the way.

But courting Katy had been different from pursuing his other goals in life.

His thoughts were interrupted by a familiar masculine chuckle.

"Getting restless, Garrett? I wondered how long you and my daughter would stick around to enjoy the party. I can't blame you for starting to think about leaving. It's nearly nine o'clock, and you've got an hour's drive ahead of you if you're going to get to that hotel over on the coast tonight. Wilma tells me Katy picked the honeymoon spot?"

Garrett nodded briefly at his new father-in-law. "That's right. I told her to handle that end of things along with the wedding plans. Not really my field of expertise."

Harry Randall grinned knowingly. "Definitely women's work."

Garrett liked Harry Randall. When he had first gone to work for him years ago, Randall had been the wealthiest man Garrett had ever met. Since then he had met a number of men who controlled a great deal more money than Randall did, but Garrett hadn't met any he liked or respected as much as he did Harry Randall.

It wasn't just that Randall had given him that all-important job years ago when Garrett had been running wild and looking for trouble. Garrett also respected Randall professionally. He had learned a lot working in the Randall stables. Randall knew most of what there was to know about breeding techniques, auctions and show rings. He was an expert stud-farm manager, and many of the management techniques Garrett had learned back then had been directly applicable to other areas of ranching and farming.

Randall was a strong, raw-boned man whose dark hair had turned gray over the years and whose athletic build was still surprisingly intact.

Harry Randall, was, in fact, an excellent match for his tall, striking wife, Wilma. She, too, had maintained a good figure by dint of daily riding and was still active in the show ring, where she sat regally atop the beautiful Randall Arabians. Wilma was also a brilliant hostess, a skill that had considerable value in a world where people who spent thousands of dollars on horses expected a certain amount of pampering and attention.

"I'm going to miss my daughter, Garrett. Best breeding-program manager I've ever had. She had a real talent for the business. You're getting one heck of a smart business partner."

"I know," Garrett admitted.

Harry smiled genially. "Well, I can hardly complain, can I? After all, I may be losing a manager, but I'm gaining a son-in-law. I was a bit startled to see you when you showed up a few months back, but I wasn't altogether surprised by what you'd done with your life. I always knew you had what it takes to make it on your own."

"You gave me a hand when I needed it, Harry. I won't ever forget that."

"I got my money's worth out of you," Harry said with a chuckle. "You worked harder than any stable boy I've ever had, except maybe my own daughter. I remember how she used to hang around you when you took that job with us. She was just a kid, but I think she was half in love with you then. When I saw the way she looked at you when you walked back into our lives a few months ago, I knew how the wind was blowing. And you weren't trying to run in the opposite direction, were you?"

Garrett's teeth flashed in one of his rare grins. "No, sir, I wasn't doing any running."

"Everything all set at your new place?"

Garrett nodded, his tone turning instantly serious. It was important that Harry Randall knew Garrett would do right by his daughter. "Don't worry. Your daughter will have a proper home. It's a big house, a little like your own. Sits on a bluff with a view of the ocean. Lots of land around it. Used to be a lot more land, but the owner began selling off parcels a few years back. Now there's just a stable and paddock, although the stable building needs some work. I'm having my old quarter horse, Red Dazzle, moved there as soon as it's ready. I've got him on some rental pasture now."

"You said someone's been living on the place?"

Garrett nodded. "There's a caretaker and his wife. They've been living there for years. I gather they were loyal to the original owner and didn't have anyplace to go when he sold to me. I more or less inherited them, but that's all right. I need a handyman, and I want Katy to have a housekeeper. You and Wilma will have to come visit us soon."

"Thanks, Garrett, we'll look forward to the visit. But we won't rush it. Newlyweds need a little time to themselves. Speaking of time, Katy tells me you've arranged to take a couple of weeks off for the honeymoon?"

Garrett nodded. "I figured we could both use the time to settle in to the new house, and I want to get Red's stable in shape. There's a lot to do. The caretaker has let a few things go. Not much incentive to keep everything in shape, I guess. He wasn't certain the new owner would even want him to stay on. As far as the house goes, I haven't spent a night there myself. The interior designer just got finished last week, and I had my personal belongings moved just before I came down here for the wedding."

"I know Katy is looking forward to seeing her new home." Harry smiled fondly across the room to where Katy stood talking to a small group of well-wishers. His eyes darkened into a familiar seriousness.

"Don't worry about her, Harry," Garrett said in response to the unspoken question. "I'll take good care of her."

"I know you will, Garrett. But it's still a little strange, you know. Gives a man a funny feeling to see his little girl get married. Do me a favor, will you?"

Garrett looked at him. "What's that?"

"Try to get her back in a saddle one of these days."

"I understood she hasn't ridden in years. Wilma said Katy will never get on a horse again."

"Katy used to be beautiful in a saddle," Harry Randall said a bit wistfully. "Even when she was a little girl. Remember? When she took a horse into the show ring, she dominated the place. Every eye was on her and the horse she was riding. She had a way of making that particular animal look like the most important horse in the entire known world. What's more, she made the horse feel the same way. She won ribbons on animals I wouldn't bother to take out on a Sunday walk. Somehow when she was with them, they turned into champions. An amazing talent, and all of it gone to waste because of what happened the night of that damned barn fire."

"She was badly hurt, wasn't she?" Garrett asked, his eyes on his wife. He remembered how much she had loved riding when she was a kid. He'd lost count of the number of times he had tossed her up into the tiny, elegant English saddles she always used. When she'd cantered into a show ring, she almost always came out with more than her share of ribbons. Harry Randall was right—Katy had come alive when she was on a horse.

"Yes, she was badly hurt," Harry said softly. "But more than that, she was badly scared. So scared she's refused to ride again."

"Is Katy's limp a leftover from the injuries she received in that fire?" Garrett asked. Katy had never talked about what had happened that night. Garrett had picked up bits and pieces of the story from others.

"She was nearly killed trying to get the horses out." Harry's voice was suddenly grim. "She was leading the last one to safety when a burning timber fell right in the path of the horse. The animal was already on the verge of panic. The falling timber was the last straw. The blindfold came off and the horse went wild. A big, heavy stallion. Katy didn't have a chance of controlling him. The stallion knocked her down and trampled her in his effort to escape the fire."

"Who got her out?" Garrett asked tightly. It was the first time he had heard the full story.

"I did," Harry said simply. "I hadn't even realized she was inside the barn until someone told me she was missing. I found her unconscious, lying there in the dirt and the smoke. The flames were starting to explode around her. I found her and carried her out, and when she came to in a hospital bed she told me she would never ride again. The fear and the pain did something to her."

"She lost her nerve when it came to horses," Garrett concluded. "You should have made her get back into a saddle the minute she came out of the hospital."

Harry shook his head. "I couldn't do it. She wasn't a child. She was twenty years old and she had been severely traumatized. She made up her mind never to ride again and that was that. The fear in her eyes when she even thought about riding after that was more than enough to keep me from trying to force her to do anything. But maybe one of these days you'll be able to convince her to get back on a horse. Husbands can sometimes accomplish things fathers can't."

"What makes you think I could get her to do something you and her mother haven't been able to get her to do?" Garrett asked with genuine curiosity.

Harry shrugged. "I don't know," he said softly. "It's something about the way she looks at you. I think my daughter is very much in love."

Garrett thought about that. "Good," he said finally. "That'll make things simpler."

# 2

THE BIGGEST MISTAKE OF HER LIFE.

Katy sat staring out the window of Garrett's white Mercedes and tried to tell herself that her fears were groundless. Her bridal jitters would vanish now that the stress of the wedding and reception were behind her. She had worked very hard during the past few weeks to ensure that everything went exactly as planned.

The wedding had been picture perfect, an elaborate, formal ceremony followed by a joyous, no-expense-spared celebration. No bride could have wished for more. But perhaps this particular bride had worked a little too hard and was now paying the price. The stressful part was over. She was alone with her husband at last. She could relax.

But the truth was she could detect no real improvement in her mood. Her nerves felt raw and jumpy, her stomach was tied in knots and she was experiencing a strange sensation that seemed to hover somewhere between fear and wild panic. She had to get a grip on herself. She would not allow herself to have a full-scale anxiety attack on her wedding night.

"Are you okay, Katy?" Garrett slanted his wife a quick, assessing glance as he skillfully steered the car along the coastal highway. The road was shrouded in darkness. An invisible sea pounded on the cliffs below the curving highway. "You look a little tense."

"Getting married turned out to be more stressful than I had imagined," she admitted with a determinedly cheerful smile. "The whole thing doesn't seem to have bothered you much, though. I thought weddings made men nervous, not women."

Garrett shrugged, his shoulders moving easily beneath his expensive white shirt. His jacket had been tossed impatiently onto the back seat earlier when he had climbed behind the wheel, and he had loosened his tie before he'd started the car. It was obvious Garrett had merely been tolerating the formal clothes he had been obliged to wear. "A wedding is just something a man goes through to get to the other side. No point getting worked up about one. A wedding is nothing more than a formality."

"A very pragmatic thought." Katy wondered if he had heard the underlying sarcasm in her voice. Probably not, she decided. Garrett wouldn't be expecting any sarcasm from her. She was almost never sharp-tongued, least of all with him. She leaned her head back against the headrest and contemplated the hours of planning, preparation and decision making she had put into the elaborate event he had just labeled a mere "formality." The task of arranging the perfect wedding had consumed her for weeks.

"You're tired," Garrett told her, as if that explained her unfamiliar mood to his satisfaction.

"I suppose so." She didn't feel tired, however. She felt keyed up and on edge, as though she were waiting for the other shoe to drop.

"Why don't you try to nap until we reach the hotel?"

"I can't sleep in a car."

"Try."

"I said," she repeated, spacing each word out carefully, "I can't sleep in a car."

"All right," Garrett said calmly, "why don't you talk instead? You haven't said more than a handful of words since we left the reception."

Katy drew a deep, steadying breath and blinked away a hint of painful moisture from her eyes. She was acting like an idiot. Nothing was wrong. She was married to the man she loved and he was trying to conduct a pleasant conversation as they approached the intimacy of their wedding night. She must calm down and relax. Everything was all right.

"It was a lovely reception, wasn't it?" Katy tried to sound relaxed and casual.

"Uh-huh," Garrett replied absently, his mind clearly on other matters. "You know, honey, I'm anxious for you to see your new home. You're going to like it. It fits you."

"I'm looking forward to seeing it," Katy said politely.

Garrett was momentarily reflective, unusual for him. "Maybe I should have let you see the place before I bought it."

"You bought the place before you asked me to marry you," Katy reminded him, mildly amused by his mood of momentary doubt. She knew it wouldn't last long. Garrett was invariably very sure of himself. "In fact, you'd already hired the craftspeople and the interior designer before you even mentioned that you'd bought a house. There wasn't any opportunity for me to get involved in the process."

Garrett frowned, his short flicker of uncertainty vanishing quickly. "I couldn't wait for the deal. When

Atwood finally decided to sell, I had to act immediately. I couldn't risk losing the place. As far as the interior design part was concerned, I already knew what I wanted."

"I know." Katy half smiled to herself. "You told me you wanted a home that looked like my parents' home."

Garrett nodded. "I like that Southwestern stuff. It suits me and it suits you. You're going to be happy in your new home."

"I'm sure the designer did a fine job." Katy's brief flash of amusement disappeared. Now she wanted to cry. This was her wedding night. If she and Garrett were going to talk, they should be talking about themselves, not the work the interior designer had done. Normally Garrett's enthusiasm for his new property charmed and delighted her. His desire to create a real home of his own was touching. But tonight she couldn't summon the sense of anticipation she usually felt when she talked about such things with Garrett. She wanted him to talk to her on a more personal level.

"I was telling your dad there's still some work to be done on the stables before I have Red Dazzle delivered, but I don't think it will take too long to get one of the stalls in shape. I've got Bracken, the caretaker who's been living on the place, to help me."

"I'm looking forward to meeting the Brackens." Katy tried to keep her voice neutral. She propped her elbow on the door and leaned her head against her hand. The darkness outside seemed endless.

"Like I told you a few weeks ago, if they don't work out, we can let them go. But I felt more or less obliged to keep them on and give them a chance after I closed the deal with Silas Atwood. Atwood gave me this long story about how they'd been with his family since the year one, and he didn't want to see them dumped on the street."

"It was nice of him to be concerned."

"It was the only thing he was concerned about," Garrett said. "That and not selling to his neighbor, Royce Hutton. Hutton had been after Atwood for years to sell him the last strip of Atwood land, but old Silas didn't like Hutton."

"Any particular reason?" Katy asked, not really caring.

"Hutton and Atwood's sons were friends. When Atwood's boy was killed in a fall several years ago, Hutton was one of the boys with him. From what I could gather, Atwood never forgave any of the kids who had been with his son that night, even though what happened was an accident."

"I see. Well, I'm anxious to see the place." Katy tried to inject a little more enthusiasm into her voice. What was wrong with her tonight? Most of her conversations with Garrett were about his plans for his consulting business, her role in that business or the land and house he had recently bought outside of San Luis Obispo. She had told herself time and again that Garrett wasn't the type of man who found it easy to talk about more intimate subjects.

During the past couple of months Katy had thought she and Garrett were growing close. Beneath their shared interests lay the promise of another kind of sharing. Katy had been deeply aware of the physical attraction between them almost from the start. The adolescent hero worship she had experienced in her youth was nothing compared to the rush of excitement that had materialized the day Garrett Coltrane had reappeared at the Randall Stud Farm.

It wasn't that she had spent the intervening years missing him. She had been busy showing her father's Arabians until her accident. Then she had become totally involved with her studies at college. Later she had immersed herself in her work. In fact, in recent years, she had only occasionally thought of Garrett and wondered what had become of him. But the day he'd walked back into her life a couple of months ago, it was as if her old, childish emotions had been in hibernation for years. They'd leaped into life, and this time they were no longer adolescent fantasies. They were full-blooded passions of a mature woman.

She had told herself Garrett was as aware of the physical attraction between the two of them as she was. Katy had assured herself he felt the same emotions she did. It was just unfortunate that the logistics of their situation had made it impossible to give full rein to their feelings until tonight. Besides, Garrett was not a man to rush matters. He did things in his own way and in his own time.

*The strong silent type.* How many times had she privately pinned that label on him, she wondered.

During the past two months she had been the subject of a very proper, very polite courtship conducted under the eyes of her parents and everyone else in town. But it had also been a very definite, very determined courtship. Katy had been happy enough to surrender to the joy of being courted by Garrett Coltrane, but she had once or twice wondered what would have happened if she hadn't been so willing. Somehow she wasn't at all certain the conclusion would have been any different. Garrett had learned how to get what he wanted in recent years.

It had not been a particularly romantic sort of courtship, Katy reflected. Garrett wasn't the kind of man who brought flowers or wrote poetry. He hadn't even tried to take the intimate side of the relationship too far, even though she had offered no resistance. He had kissed her, certainly, but there had been a certain restraint in all his displays of affection.

Katy had told herself that Garrett's physical remoteness was a very admirable, very endearing aspect of his nature. Most men these days were not so concerned about sexual restraint. They wanted to climb all over a woman and feel free to walk away the next morning with no sense of commitment. She had been deeply appreciative of Garrett's approach because she was the shy type herself. Her nature was warm and giving, but she definitely did not want to be pushed too quickly into a physical relationship. She was the kind of woman who needed time.

Well, she'd had time—too much time. Time enough to start developing a few doubts. Now her wedding night was upon her.

Perhaps Garrett had found it easy to restrain himself during the past few weeks for the simple reason that he wasn't all that interested in making love to her.

Perhaps he wasn't in love with her at all.

Katy knew that, objectively speaking, Leonora Bates had been right. Garrett had something to gain from a marriage to Katy Randall, something he hadn't had most of his life. Respectability, acceptance, and social connections were all reasons for a man to marry a particular woman. So, too, was proving something to himself. By marrying Katy, Garrett had made it clear that he really had pulled himself up by his bootstraps. He was now a force to be reckoned with. He had transformed himself from a no-account stable boy into a man who could ask for and get the hand of his former employer's daughter in marriage. Garrett Coltrane had come a long way. Marrying Katy Randall proved that fact to anyone who cared to look.

It gave Katy cold chills now to think that Garrett might have married her as a way of proving something to himself and the world.

She had to be wrong. Her future happiness depended on her fears being totally false.

Just a bad case of bridal jitters, she reassured herself.

But soon she would know the truth, Katy realized. She would know how Garrett really felt when he made love to her. Surely a man wouldn't hide his true feelings from a woman during the intimate act of love.

By dawn all her questions and doubts would be resolved one way or the other.

AN HOUR AND A HALF LATER Katy lay beneath the fluffy covers of a wide bed in the honeymoon suite she had selected and waited for Garrett to emerge from the bathroom. When she heard the shower stop, she put out a hand and switched off the bedside lamp. The romantic room was immediately concealed in darkness. Katy felt more comfortable in the shadows.

She had chosen this hotel and this suite from a brochure. It was one of many brochures she had collected after Garrett had casually put her in charge of finding a place to spend their wedding night. The photo in the pamphlet hadn't lied. The suite was indeed all pink and silver and white and frilly and romantic. There was a mirror in the canopy that covered the circular bed, champagne in a silver bucket and a bowl of exotic fruit on the table in front of the window. There was even a fireplace set in one wall. Pink toweling robes labeled His and Hers hung in the bathroom.

Katy had been forced to stifle a nervous giggle when Garrett had first stalked into the room behind the bell-boy. He had stood staring in astonishment at the fantasy that surrounded him. The contrast was outrageous. He was hard and dark and utterly male and the room was frothy and pink and quite feminine. He looked like a free-roaming stallion that had somehow found himself locked up in a boudoir.

"How in the hell did you find this place?" he had demanded ruefully as he'd tipped the grinning bellboy and dismissed him.

"It wasn't easy," Katy had assured him. "I went through a lot of brochures before I discovered the one advertising this particular suite."

Garrett had stared at her in chagrined amazement. "You mean you knew it looked like this when you made the reservations?"

Katy's momentary flash of amusement had faltered. "I thought it looked romantic in the picture."

Garrett had looked as if he wanted to say a great deal more on the subject, but something had stopped him. He had gallantly swallowed the rest of his outrage, glanced meaningfully at his watch and suggested gently that Katy use the bathroom first.

When she had come hesitantly out of the bathroom in her expensive new peignoir, she had found Garrett pacing back and forth across the pink carpet. He had stopped abruptly when she appeared, and his eyes had skimmed over her silk-draped figure with a degree of hunger that was startling. Katy realized she was too accustomed to his restraint. Then, with a brief, surprisingly gentle smile, he had vanished into the bathroom.

Now she was waiting for him, and it seemed easier to wait in darkness.

He loved her, Katy thought forcefully. He had to love her. She couldn't have misjudged him completely. The problem was simply that he wasn't the type of man who was good with words of intimacy. But when he came out of the bathroom and made love to her, she would be reassured. Her doubts would be put to rest once and for all.

In the bathroom Garrett dried himself quickly, fiercely aware of the sexual tension that now gripped his entire body. He couldn't remember ever feeling that much throbbing sensual anticipation. The ache in his loins was almost painful. It was as if an invisible barrier that had been in place for the past two months had crumbled completely today.

For the past eight weeks he had been thinking of a hundred different things, of his new home, of the future of his business, of how well Katy would suit him, of how satisfying it was to have Harry Randall's approval. Garrett knew he had been thinking of everything except about what it really meant to be marrying sweet, gentle, tractable Katy Randall.

Tonight he was no longer thinking of anything else except the most personal, intimate side of marriage, and the results of that thinking were evident in the pulsating hardness of his body. He felt as if he were suddenly and without any warning at the edge of his self-control.

His fingers shook slightly as he opened the bathroom door.

Garrett stood for a moment in the doorway, a towel draped loosely around his waist, and blinked to accustom his eyes to the unexpected darkness.

Then he smiled to himself as he realized what the absence of light meant. He should have known Katy was going to be shy at this stage.

"Hey," he said softly as he moved forward into the room. "Are you out there somewhere, honey?" His bare feet sank deeply into the carpeting.

"I'm here," Katy whispered from the bed.

He heard the nervousness in her voice and instantly wanted to soothe her. "I thought maybe you'd been turned into pink candy floss by some mysterious force in this room."

"Not quite. Maybe by morning the transformation will be complete." She sounded a bit more relaxed, as if his small attempt at humor had reassured her. "You'll wake up next to a big wad of sticky cotton candy."

Garrett grinned to himself. At least she hadn't frozen up completely on him. He halted beside the bed and stood looking down at her. He wasn't sure he would have known what to do if her natural shyness had caused her to panic and go ice cold.

She was just a little nervous, he told himself. It was only natural. Hell, he was feeling a bit strange himself. A tense, restless desire was beginning to pour through him. It was as if something in him had recognized that the waiting was over. After all these years, everything was at last over. After all these years, everything was at last in place. He had his business, his home and his woman. His future was waiting for him to claim it.

Slowly he sat down on the edge of the bed and looked at his new wife as she lay waiting for him in the shadows.

Now that his eyes had adjusted to the darkness he could see her more clearly in the pale light filtering through the curtains. Her hair was as he had imagined it would be, a dark, silky fan that framed her face on the pillow. The dim light washed out the color of her eyes but he could see the intense, questioning expression in them as she gazed up at him. There was a small, uncertain smile playing about her mouth. He wanted to soothe her, gentle her, make her relax so that she could fully enjoy the passion that was about to blossom between them. He groped for unfamiliar words.

"You looked good today," he said.

"Thank you. So did you."

So much for compliments. They obviously weren't his forte. He wondered what else a new bride might like to hear. Garrett rummaged around inside his head for something that would be reassuring and encouraging.

"I forgot to ask if you might be hungry. You didn't eat much at the reception. There's fruit over there on the table."

"I'm not hungry," she replied gently.

So much for the topic of food. Maybe he shouldn't be worrying about making reassuring conversation now. After all, they weren't kids. He and Katy both knew what was supposed to happen next. But Garrett still felt an illogical need to wipe away some of the tension he sensed in his new bride. There was still something in her eyes that made him uneasy.

"We could open the champagne," he suggested, glancing at the silver bucket. The ice inside had just about melted.

"If that's what you want," Katy said politely.

Garrett's mouth tightened. "No, I don't want any. Not now." Enough of this nonsense, he told himself. Maybe it would be easier to communicate in a more fundamental manner. Garrett stood up abruptly and let the pink towel drop to the plush carpet. Without a word he pulled back the covers and slid in beside Katy. He could feel the warmth of her slender, gently curved body immediately. His whole body ached to claim that warmth. Without any further hesitation he reached out to take his bride in his arms.

"Katy, you feel good," he grated thickly as she came willingly to him.

"So . . . so do you," she whispered against his shoulder.

Garrett didn't see any further need for casual conversation. He wasn't much good at it, anyway. His body was throbbing with the force of his need, and he was sure now that Katy wanted him, too. She might be shy but she certainly wasn't fighting him. In fact, she snuggled close, responding to the pressure of his hand on the small of her back.

Garrett fumbled for a few minutes with the nightgown and then lost patience.

"This is worse than trying to get a bridle on a saddle bronc. Why do women wear such complicated things to bed?" he asked as he finally grabbed the hem of the gown and swept the whole, frothy garment up toward Katy's head.

"I thought it looked romantic," she mumbled through the folds of the material.

"It's a nuisance."

"What should I have worn? A horse blanket?"

Garrett frowned in the darkness, wondering if she had taken offense. Instantly he was contrite. "The nightgown's pretty enough, I guess."

"Like me?"

That startled him. "What's that supposed to mean?"

"Am I pretty enough for you?"

"What a crazy thing to say! Of course you're pretty enough." This was getting outrageous. He didn't understand her peculiar mood. She had been acting strangely since the wedding. Garrett leaned over and kissed her, anxious to stop the odd words and the even stranger tone. "Katy, honey, you're all I want tonight. You're beautiful."

As soon as his mouth covered hers, a part of him relaxed. She responded at once, her lips soft and pliant beneath his own. Garrett groaned as he deepened the kiss. His hand slipped eagerly over her nude body, finding and enjoying the sweet curves of hip and thigh.

Katy's arms stole around his neck. He heard her whisper something against his mouth but he didn't catch the words. He urged her lips apart, eager to taste the exciting warmth of her. His body stirred, seeking hers with a swift, consuming hunger. Garrett knew that he wouldn't be able to wait very long before he slaked that hunger in Katy's soft warmth. He couldn't remember ever needing a woman as badly as he needed Katy tonight. Somewhere within him a dam that had been in place for months had burst.

Beneath the covers he stroked Katy and felt a jolt of satisfaction when she moaned softly and pressed against him.

Her small cry sent euphoric tremors through Garrett. She was reacting so beautifully to his touch. It surprised him, but it also pleased him as nothing else ever had. His fingers glided over her breasts and paused briefly when her nipples went taut.

The lure was irresistible. Garrett reluctantly freed Katy's mouth and lowered his head to taste the hard berries he had aroused. Katy shivered when his tongue circled the peaks of her swelling breasts. Garrett was enthralled by the reaction.

"So sweet," he muttered.

His hand went lower as he eagerly searched for the soft, shadowed thicket that shielded Katy's most intimate secrets. She gasped as he found it, stiffening slightly as though afraid he would handle her roughly. She should know him better than that, Garrett thought. He would never hurt her.

"Take it easy, honey," he whispered. "Relax. Just relax and let me touch you. Lord, you're warm. And so soft." He found the tender dampening womanflesh between her legs and closed his hand around her.

Her fingers clenched in his hair, and her body arched beneath him in sudden, wild abandon. She was a sweet, even-tempered well-bred, well-mannered little mare who was suddenly showing him that she had a sensual, spirited side to her nature. Garrett hadn't expected it, and the new knowledge he was gaining about his wife sent the blood pounding through his veins.

He wanted her; wanted her with a hot, sweeping passion that was totally new to him. He couldn't remember ever having felt quite like this. No woman had ever given herself to him this freely, no woman had ever clung to him with so much urgency. He wanted nothing more than to bury himself in the velvet-lined sheath he was preparing. The small cries Katy was making against Garrett's perspiration-damp skin assured him she was as eager as he was.

Unable to wait any longer, Garrett moved onto her, aware that he was trembling with the effort it took to keep from forging into her too quickly. He could feel his muscles bunching in his shoulders and tightening across his stomach as he struggled to keep a grip on the last shreds of his self-control. He was shuddering the way a stallion shuddered in the presence of a mare. Garrett felt the same primitive wildness coursing through himself. It made him light-headed and filled him with a sense of raw masculine power. At the same time he longed to give Katy the same kind of pleasure he was soon going to be feeling.

"Part your legs, honey," he said through his teeth as he came down on top of Katy's soft, welcoming body. "Part your legs for me. Let me come inside. I want you."

Katy's hands tightened around him, her fingernails digging into his skin and setting off new sparks of electric excitement. She shyly opened her thighs for him, and Garrett groaned as he reached down to guide himself into her warmth.

Katy's small intake of breath was accompanied by a tightening of her whole body as Garrett thrust heavily into her. Her muscles constricted as if in protest and Garrett went still, aware of how small and tight she was. He must not hurt her. He must make this good for her. Maybe he'd already ruined things by pushing too fast.

"Garrett, oh, Garrett my darling, I love you so much," Katy murmured, clinging to him as if her life depended on it.

Garrett closed his eyes in an overwhelming sense of relief. It was going to be all right. She still wanted him. Slowly, carefully he began to move inside her, but the instant he sensed her renewed response he felt the last of his control slip rapidly out of reach.

He clamped a possessive hand around Katy's rounded buttocks, bringing her up into the position he wanted so that he could drive as deeply as possible into her.

"I want all of you," he told her hoarsely. "I want every inch of you."

She said nothing, but she cried out again as he stroked into her. Garrett pushed his hand between their bodies, seeking the bold little nubbin of desire that was the center of her sensation. When he discovered it, he was rewarded by Katy's sudden, delicate convulsion.

She seemed to explode beneath him as she found her release. Garrett was sucked into the vortex of passion that spiraled around them both. He felt Katy surge upward, instinctively seeking the fullness of him, and he gave himself to her with a husky shout of satisfaction.

Katy was stunned by the sensation of pleasure bursting deep within her. This was what her body had been seeking for the past few minutes. She had never experienced it before, and the full impact left her breathless. Unable to do anything else, she wrapped herself tightly around Garrett and rode the shifting currents of the storm with him.

It was a long time before she came completely back to reality. She was aware that Garrett hadn't left her body. He was still lying on top of her, the weight of him pushing her into the bedding. She could feel the sheen of dampness on his skin. He felt heavy and replete.

A physically satisfied male.

Well, she could hardly complain about that, she thought. In all honesty, she was forced to admit that physically, she, too, had found satisfaction. The difference was that for Garrett this kind of satisfaction was clearly sufficient.

But as she came slowly back to reality, Katy realized it was not enough for her.

Her own words, spoken in the most intimate moments of passion came back to haunt her. *I love you.*

There had been no answering response from Garrett. Even in the depths of desire he had been unable to speak of his love.

She could no longer tell herself that he was simply the strong, silent type. After all, he had been able to speak of such things as desire and his own need. He had said excitingly rough, urgent things to her that had increased her response to him. He had told her he wanted her.

But there had been no words of love.

Katy slowly opened her eyes and looked up into the dark mirror overhead. She had to accept the truth. Whatever Garrett felt for her, it didn't include love.

She had made a terrible mistake.

Garrett shifted finally. He exhaled deeply, a long, relaxed sigh of contentment and satisfaction and then he raised his head to look down at Katy. In the shadows she could see the possessive gleam in his mouth. He stroked her tangled hair back from her cheek with an absent gesture of affection.

It was the kind of gesture, Katy told herself grimly, that he might have used with a mare who had performed especially well for him.

"You're a little new at this, aren't you?" he asked equably.

In her overly sensitive state of mind, Katy wondered if the comment was meant as a mild insult. Perhaps she hadn't performed all that well. She stiffened slightly beneath him, but Garrett didn't seem to notice.

"A little," she said cautiously.

He nodded, apparently not too put out by the information. "I thought so."

"Was I that bad?"

He looked shocked at the question and at the underlying vehemence. His big hands cradled her face with unexpected urgency. "What the hell are you talking about now? It was great. All of it. I've never felt—" He broke off abruptly. "Forget it. I was completely satisfied and I had the impression you were, too. Don't try to deny it, honey."

"I'm not denying it."

"Good." He appeared relieved. He rolled onto his back, cradling her against him. "I guess a woman like you is bound to be somewhat high-strung on her wedding night."

"Is that right?"

"Sure, and I can understand it." He made a sweeping, magnanimous gesture with one hand. "You're kind of quiet by nature. You always were. You haven't exactly led a wild life since I last saw you, have you, honey?"

"No," she agreed coolly, "I haven't. Compared to your life, I imagine mine must seem rather dull."

"No, it doesn't. It seems warm and safe and comfortable. I'm glad you've been safe and secure all these years. You're not the type to try for the fast lane."

The thought that he found her inability to fit into the fast lane amusing fueled the dangerous mixture of emotions that were beginning to simmer in Katy. "I haven't exactly been living in a locked box, you know. I have plenty of friends and a reasonably active social life."

"Hey, calm down, I didn't say you'd been living in total seclusion."

He tried soothing her with a slow stroking motion that only made Katy think of the techniques he used to soothe horses. She remembered well that Garrett had always been good with horses. He'd handled animals in her father's stables that no one else could control. She stirred against him and tried to pull away. "Please," she whispered, "I want to go clean up."

He held her more tightly. "It's all right, you know. There's nothing to be embarrassed about. It's all natural. Go to sleep, Katy. It's been a long, tiring day and you're still riding on your nerves. Just go to sleep."

She knew she wasn't going to be able to escape the restraint of his arm without causing a major scene, so Katy lay still beside her new husband and waited for him to follow his own advice. She had a horror of scenes.

It didn't take long. Garrett was asleep within minutes.

Katy carefully slipped out from under his arm to go into the bathroom. Once inside, she shut the door and sat down on the edge of the tub to cry.

She didn't cry for long. She wasn't the type. Ten minutes later Katy wiped her eyes and made her decision.

## 3

SOMETIME AFTER ONE O'CLOCK Katy managed to crawl back into bed without disturbing Garrett and fall into a restless sleep. Garrett had been right about one thing—it had been a long, tiring day and she needed the rest.

She awoke shortly before dawn, coming alert with an unnatural abruptness. She knew a brief sense of disorientation until, with a jolt of adrenaline, she registered the fact that she wasn't alone in the wide bed.

Of course she wasn't alone. Garrett was beside her. She had married a man who didn't love her but who now had the right to sleep with her.

Slowly Katy pushed aside the covers. She sat up carefully, not wanting to awaken her husband. Her beautiful nightgown was in a crumpled heap on the floor beside the bed, a pool of silver on a carpet of pink. Katy reached for the robe of the peignoir and pulled it around herself.

In the light of an approaching dawn the wedding suite appeared frivolous to the point of being ridiculous. Katy winced as she looked around. The place could give a person cavities just from looking at it. It was as phony and full of illusion as her marriage. En route to the bathroom, Katy noticed that there was nothing but water left in the ice bucket. The champagne would be warm. But that hardly mattered.

Women such as she did not drink champagne for breakfast. Only fast-living types got to do that sort of thing. Katy barely resisted the urge to pick up the bucket and hurl the contents at Garrett's unsuspecting head.

By the time she had emerged from the bathroom dressed in jeans and a green top, the sun was just barely above the horizon. A glance at the bed showed Garrett still apparently asleep. Katy glared at his motionless figure sprawled beneath the pink-and-white-striped sheet. The man hadn't even noticed that his bride was missing from his side, she thought resentfully. She stalked to the window.

It took her a moment to identify the emotions she was experiencing. Katy had not had a lot of experience with such things as resentment, anger and outrage.

Outside, sunlight played on the Pacific, changing the color of the ocean into an intense blue that stretched to the end of the world. Katy gazed out at the endless vista and wondered at the force of the anger that blazed within her. She had never felt like this before in her life. It was as startling in its own way as the discovery of the depths of her own passionate nature had been last night.

Garrett Coltrane, she reflected furiously, was the cause of both new experiences. For some reason that only made her angrier.

"Morning, honey." Garrett's voice came from behind her, rich and husky with sleep and what sounded suspiciously like remembered satisfaction. "You're up bright and early. Get enough rest?"

"I'm fine, Garrett." Katy kept her eyes on the view outside the window.

"You're already dressed. What's the rush? We've got plenty of time. Why don't you take off those jeans and hop back into bed?"

Katy seethed. "Now, why on earth would I want to do that?" she asked very softly without turning around. "Give me one good reason."

There was a slight pause behind her as if Garrett was finally beginning to sense that all was not quite as he had assumed it would be that morning.

"You want a reason?" he asked blandly, "How about because this is the morning after our wedding and new brides usually want to spend a little extra time in bed. So do grooms." He spoke carefully, obviously feeling his way. The sheets rustled slightly as he pushed them aside.

"What would you know about the behavior of new brides and grooms? Have you been married very many times?"

"No, I haven't been married before and you know it. Katy, what's wrong?" He stood up and started toward her.

Katy could hear him padding barefoot across the carpet. She was afraid to turn around, afraid to see the whole of him in the light of day. He was strong enough and powerful enough to affect her senses in darkness. She didn't want to have to deal with the full force of him in daylight. Not yet.

"Katy?" He sounded impatient now.

"You don't love me." She spoke without moving and she knew her words had halted him, too.

"Hell, Katy, ever since the wedding, you've been saying the damnedest things. What's the problem here?"

"The problem," she repeated as if he were a slow-witted mule, "is that you don't love me."

He took a deep breath, clearly striving for patience and understanding. Both were, apparently, alien. "Katy, I don't know what's gotten into you. You're not making much sense. Nothing has changed between us since yesterday or last week or last month, for that matter. Everything is going just as we planned. I feel the same way about you as I did when I asked you to marry me."

"I know." Her voice was laced with disgust.

"Then why in hell are you so upset?" He sounded honestly confused.

"It's not your fault."

"Well, that's a relief," he retorted. "Mind telling me who is to blame and exactly what he or she is being blamed for?"

Katy's fingers clenched around a fistful of curtain. "It's my fault," she said starkly. "I'm to blame. I misjudged you, your feelings and the whole situation. I thought you loved me. Do you hear me? I was stupid enough to think you loved me. I thought you just had trouble saying the words. I thought the only problem," she added scathingly, "was that you were the strong, silent type. Isn't that a joke?" She spun around to confront him, and her treacherous left ankle collapsed beneath her, pitching her forward.

Instantly Garrett was there, gliding to catch her in his arms before she hit the floor. "Take it easy," he muttered, steadying her. "Calm down, honey. You're going to hurt yourself. Just take it easy." His voice was the familiar, soothing rumble he used to quiet a horse.

Katy shut her eyes in an agony of fury and humiliation. She swore bluntly, using a four-letter word she knew Garrett had never heard her use before in all the time he had known her. As she found her balance, she jerked free of his grasp. She stumbled a little as she righted herself, but she stayed upright when she reached out to catch hold of the edge of the table. Using it as a prop, she faced him once more. Her eyes were brilliant with the force of her emotions.

"It finally dawned on me yesterday that I might have made the biggest mistake of my life. During the past week I got more and more uncertain, but I kept telling myself all brides were nervous. Yesterday I decided I was just suffering a bad case of bridal jitters. But the truth was, I wasn't willing to admit to myself that I had been so wrong about you. But last night I had to face the truth."

Garrett stared at her as if she'd taken leave of her senses. He appeared totally unconcerned with his own nudity. His body was lean and powerful in the morning light as he faced her with his legs braced. His eyes glittered with annoyance and a growing frustration.

"Last night," he said, "the only truth you had to face was the fact that you're a very sensual woman. I fail to see what's so devastating about that. From all outward appearances, you liked what you found in my arms."

Katy's anger leaped into a bright flame. "I'm not talking about sex, I'm talking about love. I did not find love in your arms last night, Garrett. The sex isn't much good without it."

The first traces of real anger appeared in his eyes. "What happened between us last night was damned good. Don't try to deny it."

Katy threw up her hands in a gesture of frustrated fury. "Why am I even bothering to argue with you? You don't understand. You never will understand. You married me because I'm Katy Randall. Because you like my father. Because I'm an expert on breeding programs. Because you had reached the point in your life when you wanted to add a wife to your list of possessions."

Garrett raked his fingers through his dark hair. He was still making a bid for patience. "You're right about one thing; I don't understand you. Katy, during the whole time we've been seeing each other seriously during the past couple of months you've been a reasonable, sensible woman. You and I have a lot in common. We've known each other for years. Your father approves of me. We're physically attracted to each other. What more do you want? No one forced you to marry me. You seemed to want it as much as I did. I just don't understand what's wrong with you this morning."

"Last night I told you I loved you," she said, hating to have to repeat the words.

His expression softened. "I know," he said gently. "You were very sweet last night."

She ignored him. "You didn't bother to respond."

"Not respond! Lady, I made love to you."

"That doesn't count."

It was Garrett's turn to swear. He did so, forcefully. "What did you want from me? Some kind of flowery, mushy love poem in the middle of the night? If that's what you were expecting, then you're more naive than I thought."

"All I wanted," Katy said, "was to be told that you loved me, too. I wanted some reassurance that I had made the right decision."

"You *did* make the right decision. Ours is going to be a good marriage. At least it will be as soon as you settle down and stop carrying on like a filly who's just had a saddle put on her back for the first time."

It was all Katy could do to keep herself from throwing something at him. She lifted her head and pinned him with her eyes. "Are you saying I was wrong? That I'm upset over nothing? Are you saying you do love me?"

He sucked in his breath but his eyes never wavered. "I'm saying that we've got everything going for us. I don't know what the hell's the matter with you this morning, but we're going to make this marriage work."

"Do you love me?"

"I want you, I respect you, I intend to take care of you," he stated with dogged determination. "I've never done anything to make you think otherwise. Christ, I didn't even take you to bed until I put a ring on your finger. I thought you'd appreciate all that gentlemanly restraint, if nothing else."

"But you don't love me."

Garrett's hard face was set in rigid lines. He was obviously fighting an internal battle as he tried to dampen his growing anger. "Don't do this to yourself, Katy. You're tearing yourself apart for no good reason."

"Just answer my question, damn you!"

Something snapped in his self-control. "All right, if you want to hear it spelled out, the answer is no, I don't love you."

Katy felt the last of her naive hope wither and die. She blinked rapidly and swallowed to get rid of the tears that were threatening to overwhelm her. Her fingers were shaking as she clamped her hand around the edge of the table to steady herself.

"I guess it's better to get the facts straight now, even if it is a little late," she whispered.

Garrett watched her through narrowed eyes. Then he took a long step forward and caught her by the arms. His fingers locked around her, and he anchored her in front of him. "You've had your say, Katy, now you're going to listen to me. There's no need to look like a foal who's just had her legs kicked out from under her the first time she tries to stand. It's not my fault you've got some fantasy notion about love and marriage. I thought you were too sensible and down-to-earth to indulge in that kind of idiocy. I thought you understood what was important and what wasn't. Love is just like this screaming pink hotel room—nothing more than a lot of pink-and-white froth that evaporates in the sun or melts in the rain."

"You don't know what you're talking about."

"I do know what I'm talking about," he gritted. "It's easy enough to say the words. Do you think I haven't heard them before? Do you think I don't know how meaningless they are? Words like love don't count, Katy. Commitment counts. Honesty counts. Compatibility counts. Sex counts."

She flinched, her eyes widening. "What do you mean, you've heard words like love before?"

"Katy, I'm thirty-five," he reminded her in exasperation. "I've had a little more experience than you have."

"Oh, I see. I'm not the first woman you've had in your bed who's told you she loves you, is that it?" she snapped.

Garrett looked exasperated. "No, you're not."

"Did you give those other women the same lecture you're giving me? Did you spell out in detail the fact that you didn't love them? Did you call them idiots for wanting all the silly pink-and-white trappings?"

"You talk as if there have been hundreds of women," he retorted gruffly. "Katy, I'm a working man. I always have been. You, of all people, know the kind of life I lead. It doesn't allow a lot of time or opportunity for an endless chain of affairs."

"Okay, forget the numbers," she shot back. "Just tell me how many of those women you loved in return."

His gaze turned very dangerous. "I only made the mistake once, and that was a long time ago. It happened after I left that job at your father's stables and hit the rodeo circuit as a pro. She was the prettiest woman I'd ever seen and she wanted me. Me, a guy who's biggest accomplishment at that point was that he'd managed to stay out of jail. A guy with no respectable family and no respectable future. I couldn't offer her more than a lot of dreams and hopes and plans. But it turned out she didn't care about things like that. She was a spoiled little rich girl who got her kicks sleeping with rodeo cowboys. Some women go for rock stars, some go for race-car drivers and some go for cowboys. Cowboys were her thing. And when she was tired of one, she dropped him and went looking for another. The thought of actually marrying some blue-collar, working-class hick who wore jeans and boots made her laugh."

"Garrett . . ."

"She said she loved me, but when I asked her to marry me, she laughed in my face. I couldn't blame her, but it taught me a lesson."

"What sort of lesson?" Katy demanded with passionate anger.

"It taught me that next time I wanted to marry a woman I would make damned certain the relationship was based on a more solid foundation than some fairytale emotion labeled love!"

"And you thought our relationship was based on something more solid and reliable than love, right?"

"Right." His fingers flexed around her arms. "I thought," he continued pointedly, "that I'd picked the right kind of woman this time, the kind of woman I needed."

"And now you find out her head is filled with just as much pink fluff as any other woman's. We've been so busy planning your future for the past few weeks that we forgot to discuss mine. A bad oversight, Garrett. Rather like buying a mare without first checking her teeth."

"Katy, stop it. You're talking nonsense. Just settle down and listen to me. I've spent all my life learning that you can't trust fancy words. My father trusted the words of the banker who let him put his ranch so deep in debt he never could get back out. The bank wound up with the ranch. My mother believed my father when he told her he was going to get rich raising cattle. My father trusted my mother to stick by him when the going got tough. They were both disappointed. Katy, pretty words don't mean anything. It's what people do that counts."

"You're wrong, Garrett. Some words are important."

"I'll give you the important ones. But I won't give you or any other woman the meaningless ones."

Katy's eyes blazed. "You're just making excuses. Maybe you're so damned macho you're afraid to let yourself fall in love. Maybe you're the kind of man who thinks he makes himself vulnerable if he tells a woman he loves her. That's not like proving yourself against a bull or a saddle bronc, is it? Falling in love means taking a *real* risk—the kind of risk I took by marrying you yesterday."

"Honey, this is crazy. You're my wife. You belong to me now. We've got a future together. It's a future we both want. Why are you trying to rip everything to shreds just because I'm not romantic enough to suit your feminine notions of how a husband is supposed to act?"

Garrett's hands tightened around her arms, and Katy suddenly sensed the physical change in him. Instinctively she glanced down. She nearly choked with fury and another equally dangerous emotion when she realized Garrett was fully, heavily aroused. It was the last straw. Hastily she turned her head to one side and stared fixedly at a picture on the wall.

"Will you please get dressed, for heaven's sake?"

"What's the matter, Katy? Don't you like knowing you have this effect on me?" There was an amused, taunting quality in his words now.

"Not particularly."

Garrett's mouth crooked slightly and he pulled her closer. His voice softened. "I don't believe you. You've been through a lot during the past few days getting ready for the wedding. You're feeling emotional and you're not thinking clearly. Let's go back to bed and start this morning out the way we should have started it in the first place."

Katy stood stiffly in his grasp, appallingly aware of the hard feel of him as he held her close. "Please, Garrett. You said you're not interested in love, well, I'm not interested in sex without it. I married you under a . . . a misapprehension. It's been a terrible misunderstanding. A horrible mistake. I'm not blaming you. You've never lied to me. I deceived myself. But the deception is over. I know where I stand now."

"Don't look so martyred. You stand with me, dammit. You made a commitment yesterday, and last night you gave yourself to me."

"Well, I'm taking myself back," she retorted, struggling to free herself from his hold.

He didn't release her. "Just what do you think you're going to do?"

"I thought it all out last night after you went to sleep. Since it's too late for an annulment, I'll have to file for divorce. It shouldn't be too complicated. I won't be making any claims on you."

"Divorce! Katy, are you out of your mind? We've got our whole future ahead of us."

"No, you've got your whole future ahead of you. I'm going to find a different future."

"The hell you are. You want everything I want. That's one of the reasons I married you."

"I married you because I loved you, not because I wanted a similar future!" she protested.

"I don't believe you. Don't tell me you aren't interested in the kind of future I intend to build."

"I had a perfectly good future at my father's stud farm. Let go of me. It's obvious I'm wasting my time trying to explain anything to you." She lifted her flaring eyes to his grim face. "I said, let go of me."

Garrett shook his head slowly, his jaw set. "There's something different about you this morning. I've never seen you like this. Ever since I've known you, you've been sweet-natured and reasonable and . . ."

"And docile and good-tempered and well-mannered and obedient, right? I responded immediately to the leading rein and a little carefully applied pressure," she concluded for him. "Just like a well-bred mare. Well, I've got news for you, Garrett Coltrane—I'm not a horse. I apologize for any inconvenience caused by the confusion. Now go put on some clothes. I have no intention of finishing this argument while you're standing there stark naked looking like a stallion who's just been introduced to the mare he's supposed to impregnate."

Garrett froze. For a moment it seemed as though he might do something drastic, but with an obvious effort he restrained himself. He glowered down into Katy's brilliant eyes and determined face for a long moment, and then he abruptly released her. With a brutal exclamation, he turned and strode toward the bathroom, snagging a pair of jeans on the way.

"All right, I'll go have a shower and get dressed. I think we both need a little time to cool down. This *discussion* has gotten totally out of hand." He paused in the doorway and sent a warming glance back over his shoulder. "But don't get any ideas of leaving while I'm in the shower. Use a few of those brains I always credited you with having and think about what you're doing. You've got my promise we're going to settle this when I get out."

Katy's mouth trembled faintly, but her gaze didn't waver. "I'm not going to run off. I know we have to make some logistical plans. We need to talk about the legal formalities, for one thing. We'll have to consult lawyers, I suppose."

Garrett cut off the remainder of her words with a short, vicious comment. "No, we are not going to consult lawyers. Just make sure you're still here when I get out of the shower. I'll tell you then just what plans we're going to make." He closed the door with an unnerving softness, leaving Katy to stare morosely at the silver-and-pink flocked wall.

Inside the bathroom Garrett met the eyes of the man in the mirror. The other guy looked ready for battle.

"Lawyers," Garrett muttered as he wrenched the shower handle. "*Lawyers.* Of all the stupid, crazy, emotional things to say. She's talking about getting a lawyer and we've only been married less than twenty-four hours."

In his wildest flights of imagination, Garrett knew he could never have envisioned the kind of morning after the wedding night that he had encountered today. Katy was normally a sweet, gentle little creature. To think he had always felt protective of her, even when she was a kid. Hell, this morning he was the one who needed protection. He'd gone to bed with a butterfly and awakened with a wildcat.

Garrett planted his hands on the rim of the sink and glared into the mirror as he waited for the shower water to heat. A pair of dangerous gold eyes stared back at him. He had to admit that the fierce gaze, combined with the dark stubble of his beard and the natural un-handsomeness of his features did not present a particularly endearing appearance. He looked like a somewhat shopworn devil. Hardly the sort of face a new bride expected to see on the first morning after her wedding.

Garrett jerked away from the mirror and stepped into the hot shower. He couldn't do much about the rough beard or the lack of good looks—they were a part of him that his bride was going to have to learn to accept.

But, dammit, he hadn't awakened with that look in his eyes. Katy's strange, irrational behavior had been responsible for it.

To think that for the past two months he'd believed the shy kid he'd once known had grown up into such a nice, levelheaded, sensible young woman. The perfect wife for him.

Garrett groaned silently as he thought about exactly what it was he had felt when he had awakened a short time ago. His body still pulsed with morning arousal. The confrontation with his wife had done nothing to alleviate it. If anything, that had only aggravated matters. Katy was the cause of the problem. Unfortunately, she was also the cure.

Garrett leaned into the hot water, letting it pound over his head and shoulders while he tried to think his way through the wholly unexpected situation in which he found himself. He felt baffled and angry, cheated in ways he couldn't put into words. In the whole time he had known her, Katy had never looked at him the way she had this morning. He realized he had grown accustomed to the seemingly bottomless well of respect and admiration and shy feminine longing he had seen in her clear gray eyes for the past two months. He was completely dumbfounded by the change in her.

Garrett opened his eyes and stared at the swan-headed, chrome-plated shower fixture in front of him. A silly, romantic doodad, that fixture. The whole blasted hotel room was a silly, romantic, flower-scented version of a film-set French boudoir.

The elaborate wedding production had surprised him. He hadn't expected Katy to go in for that kind of hoopla. But her choice of a honeymoon suite had really amazed him. It had surprised the hell out of him, in fact. This didn't seem like Katy's kind of place at all. And all that chatter about love. The woman obviously had an unexpectedly romantic streak in her nature. Garrett felt totally unprepared.

A frivolous, romantic side to Katy was something he had not allowed for when he'd made his plans.

That realization brought him up short as a new, disturbing possibility flashed into his head. Maybe this whole mess was the result of that hidden streak of romanticism in Katy. Maybe that same element in her nature had led her to expect a lot more than what she had gotten last night.

The thought was painful in the extreme. Garrett got out of the shower and reached for a towel. Slowly he began to examine the possibility that he'd really made a mess of things last night. Perhaps he'd moved too quickly. He had wanted her so badly. She had been shy but apparently willing, and she had responded beautifully. He knew from the way she had reacted that she had never experienced that kind of sensual satisfaction before in her life.

She had given herself to him wholeheartedly.

But just maybe it had all been something of a let-down for her, Garrett acknowledged uneasily.

Just maybe Katy's romanticism, coupled with her limited amount of experience, had led her to expect nothing less than an aurora borealis flaring across the bedroom ceiling, a full orchestra playing in the background and a shimmering, cascading, dazzling display of stars.

Garrett groaned. As he had told himself during the reception, he wasn't any Don Juan or Casanova. He'd hoped gentle, intelligent, even-tempered Katy would be satisfied with what she had gotten for a bedmate, but maybe she wasn't.

He shouldn't have fallen asleep right after making love to her last night. Bad mistake. Katy had apparently spent the remainder of the night wide awake telling herself she'd been shortchanged in the husband department. By morning she had worked herself into a real fit of hysterics.

But underneath the strange display of feminine emotion, Garrett knew the real Katy still lurked. The woman he had gotten to know during the past two months must still be there somewhere. He had to find a way to reach through the fireworks and retrieve the good-natured, rational, hard-working woman behind them. Desperately he tried to think of the best approach. He had to find the key to calming her down and making her see sense again.

Garrett sucked in his breath as the answer leaped to mind. It was obvious now that he'd thought of it. The key to handling Katy was to remind her of her obligations. She was fundamentally honest, a woman of integrity. It was always a mistake to use brute force on a creature as sensitive as Katy, but a little judiciously applied guilt might work wonders. All he needed was time. She was bound to return to normal sooner or later.

He hung the towel on the rack, not noticing the entwined hearts that had been embroidered on the thick terry cloth. His mind was focused on the problem at hand. He needed to buy time. He'd try for six months.

In the other room Katy sat sipping the tea she had just ordered from room service. The minutes ticked slowly past while she tried to think of the best way to make her exit from the hotel. It would probably be best to rent a car, she decided. She wouldn't go straight home. She needed to find a place to be by herself for a while. She needed time to recover from the disaster.

Twenty minutes after he'd disappeared into the bathroom, Garrett reappeared, fastening his jeans with a quick, impatient gesture. He looked up abruptly, eyes narrowed and curiously thoughtful as he spotted Katy seated near the window. Her fingers clenched around the delicate handle of the cup, but she refused to let him see how nervous she was. He hadn't put on a shirt yet, and the morning sunlight gleamed on his broad shoulders.

In spite of herself, Katy succumbed automatically to good manners. Old habits died hard, and her mother had drilled manners into her at an early age. "Would you like a cup of tea? I ordered a pot for two."

Garrett scowled briefly at the gleaming silver pot and then shrugged. "Pour me a cup. I want to talk to you."

"There's not much more to be said." Katy manipulated the pot carefully. Her fingers were still trembling, and the last thing she wanted to do was spill the hot tea all over the beveled-glass surface of the delicate white wrought-iron table.

Garrett reached down to grasp the back of one of the little pink-cushioned chairs. He spun it around and straddled it. Then he reached for the cup Katy had just finished pouring. "There's a lot more to be said, Katy. The sooner we get it said, the better."

"Such as?" Her chin came up aggressively.

"You seem to think you've been cheated by this marriage. For some reason you've decided you aren't going to get out of it what you want. I think you're wrong. I think that when you calm down you'll realize you want the same things I do. But in the meantime we've got a problem."

"That's putting it mildly."

He ignored that, plowing grimly onward. "I had a few expectations, too, you know. As of today I expected to have a wife who would help me develop a comprehensive breeding-consultation department within my company. I expected to be marrying a partner, a woman who was willing to work as hard as I was."

Katy bit her lip as the first twinges of guilt struck her. He was right. He had been cheated, too. He had gone into this marriage with his own set of expectations, and she had given him little or no warning of hers. "I know, Garrett."

He took a long swallow of tea and continued. "If you walk out on me now, you'll be leaving me in a real bind, Katy. I was counting on you. I wanted to get that department up and running during the next six months."

She stirred uneasily. "I know. But, Garrett, don't you see—"

"All I see," he said, interrupting her ruthlessly, "is that I'm left with a serious problem."

Katy was silent. Privately she thought him more than capable of handling any serious problems that came down the road, but there was no denying she was shaking up his plans. There was also no denying that in a way he was totally innocent of any accusations of cheating or manipulation. He had never pretended to be other than he was, and he had never offered more than what he intended to provide. She was the one who had built castles of sand and fallen under the spell of her own imagination.

"I was counting on having you around, Katy." Garrett's voice was rough and bleak now. "I had a lot of plans."

"Yes, but . . ."

"It would help if you could stay with me for a while," he said gently.

Katy risked a questioning glance. His tone of voice was very disturbing. "For a while?"

"Six months, Katy. That's all I'm asking. Hell, the damage is done. You're already married to me and we've spent a night together. Nothing worse can happen, right? Just stick around and give me a hand for the next few months. You can think of it as just another job. You'll be doing the same kind of work you did for your father. We'll make it official. I'll pay you a salary."

Katy's eyes widened in astonished dismay. "Six months! But, Garrett . . ."

"All right," he said wearily, as if she had just driven a terrifically hard bargain. "You win. Make it three months."

THREE MONTHS!

As she sat curled into her corner of the Mercedes, staring at the curving coastal highway unwinding ahead of her, Katy still couldn't believe she'd allowed herself to get talked into the deal. Three months of living with Garrett. Three months of living with the illusion of being his wife. The time stretched out ahead of her, an endless sentence. It was going to be sheer torture.

So why was a part of her unaccountably relieved, she asked herself with wry self-honesty. She knew the answer to that question. She loved Garrett, and even as she had told him she wanted out of the ill-starred marriage, she had been breaking up inside. Now she had a three-month reprieve. Garrett had tried to coerce her into accepting that reprieve, but the truth was, she had allowed herself to be pushed into the arrangement.

Guilt was a powerful motivator, but it wasn't strong enough to keep her with Garrett unless that was where she wanted to be. Katy knew that. Dreams were even more powerful than guilt when it came to motivation, and a part of her did not want to let go of her fantasy.

It was stupid to allow herself to start dreaming again. Nothing would change in three months. Garrett would be the same man at the end of that time as he was now: hard, determined, his eyes fixed on his own vision of a future that was run according to his rules. Under those rules he got what he wanted without having to risk himself emotionally. He was a man with no room in his life for anything as soft as love. He admitted it.

But Katy knew that in spite of her best efforts to stop it, a thread of hope was once more coiling itself into a glittering skein that could easily blind her to reality. Three months was a long time. A lot could happen in three months.

If she was very lucky.

Katy slanted a covert glance at Garrett, who was driving with his usual relaxed concentration. He had said very little since they had checked out of the hotel. He'd slipped back into his strong, silent act, Katy decided derisively. But then, she hadn't had a whole lot to say, either. The truth was, she was still feeling rather stunned by the unnerving events that had taken place last night.

"Hungry?" Garrett broke the long silence to ask.

Katy had a difficult time refocusing her thoughts. When she did so, she was astonished to discover that she actually was hungry. "A little."

"Hardly a surprise after that poor excuse for a breakfast you ate. I told you to have something more filling than a slice of toast."

"Yes, you told me. I wasn't hungry then." Katy stared sightlessly out the window.

"You mean you didn't feel like doing anything I suggested," Garrett countered with more insight than Katy had expected him to demonstrate.

Katy's mouth tilted ruefully. "That was probably a factor."

"Well, at least you admit it. Are you going to spend the next three months acting as if your whole life has been put on hold?" It was the first hint of irritation Garrett had shown since he'd won the battle in the hotel room.

"Isn't that exactly what's happened?"

"I don't see where you're any worse off now than you were working for your father. You'll be doing the same kind of job." He paused as something crossed his mind. "Almost the same kind of job," he amended.

Katy had a strong hunch Garrett had qualified the statement because he had just remembered that she was married to him and that his status as husband still carried certain marital privileges. She felt the warmth in her cheeks as memories of her wedding night returned. Garrett had a one-track mind where anything involving his future plans were concerned, but he had also proved last night that he was more than capable of focusing his attention on at least one form of short-term gratification. He had been a sensual and powerful lover during that time when he was thinking of nothing else except his new bride.

During that brief, perfect time she had spent in his arms, Katy knew herself to be enthralled. Garrett's attention had been focused entirely on her in a way it had never been before, and she had gloried in it until the magic had ended and she had faced reality. But it was obvious that Garrett saw no jolting problem with the situation that had been created. It did not faze him in the least that his actions in bed were chillingly at odds with his convictions that he had no interest in falling in love. Katy, on the other hand, was both angry and resentful that he could be such a wonderful lover to her but have no real love in his heart for her.

Now, with typical male arrogance, Garrett was assuming that she would accept her job responsibilities in the bedroom as well as in the offices of Coltrane and Company. As far as he was concerned, he had a wife and a new equine breeding-program consultant for the next three months. She hadn't found a way to set him straight yet. Her emotions were too unsettled.

Katy stole a glance at her wedding band and wondered when she would get the nerve to actually remove it. She had a hunch Garrett would hit the roof when she did. A surreptitious glance told her he was still wearing his ring.

"You think I'm behaving like an emotional idiot, don't you?" Katy asked.

He shot her an assessing look, as if judging whether or not she could handle the truth. "I don't think you're an idiot. I know you too well to believe that. You're smart, organized and efficient."

"Gosh, thanks."

He paid no attention to her sarcasm. Maybe he was getting more accustomed to it. Either that or he thought he could squelch it by ignoring it. "But you are going off the deep end over all this. You're letting a case of bridal jitters turn into a full-scale emotional circus. We both went into this marriage with our eyes open. I let you know exactly what I wanted and expected from a wife. You've admitted I never lied to you or tried to mislead you."

"What about my expectations and needs?" she asked with soft passion. "What about what I wanted from marriage?"

"I thought," he said forcefully, "that I knew what you wanted from a husband. You never gave me an inkling that I wasn't satisfactory."

"We should have talked more, I guess," Katy said, her gaze wistful.

"We did a hell of a lot of talking during the past couple of months."

"We talked about horses and breeding programs and Red Dazzle and your plans for the future. We talked about my new job in your consulting firm. We talked about your new home. But we never really talked about us—you and me. I see that now."

"When we talked about plans for the future we were talking about you and me."

"If that's so, then we have a serious communication problem, don't we?" she tossed back.

"Nothing that can't be straightened out, given time." The words came softly between his teeth.

"I don't think three months is enough time to solve the problem we have, Garrett."

"We'll get a start on it during the next couple of weeks."

"There's no need for you to pretend we're on a honeymoon for the next two weeks. As far as I'm concerned, what we have now is a business arrangement, not a marriage." Katy was rather surprised by her own assertiveness. It was as if she were actually trying to provoke him, and that was completely out of character for her. She never deliberately caused scenes, and the only time she was really assertive was when she was talking about horses. It was odd to think that her marriage might actually have changed her personality. She had always believed such things were immutable once one became an adult.

"Does it occur to you, Katy, that I have something more at stake here than just a business deal?"

Katy flashed him a look of intense curiosity. "Such as?"

"My pride, for one thing," Garrett retorted tightly.

"Oh, that." Katy lost interest in the subject.

Garrett's temper gleamed for an instant in his eyes as he slid a sidelong glance in her direction. "You may not give a damn about my pride, lady, but I sure as hell do. I do not want all my employees and friends aware of the fact that my wife changed her mind about the marriage on her wedding night. We will take the next two weeks off, just as I originally planned, and we will spent the time trying to act like newlyweds, at least when we're in front of others. Besides, I've got some work I want to do around the house and stables. I need the time. I haven't taken more than an occasional weekend off in five years."

"If you want to waste the next two weeks, that's your business." Katy leaned forward, determined to put a halt to the conversation. "Look, there's a fast-food place coming up. We can grab a meal there."

THEY ARRIVED at Garrett's new home sometime after dark. A fitful cloud cover obscured the moonlight and made it almost impossible to see any details of the property. But Katy sensed Garrett's inner satisfaction as he turned off the main road and drove along a tree-lined road that led toward the sea. He began describing the night-shrouded scene to her.

"The main house is over there on the left behind those trees. You'll see it in a moment. It's near the top of the cliffs. You're going to like it, Katy. Red tile roof, white stucco finish and lots of arched doorways and windows. Plenty of gardens, too. Over there on the right are the stables and paddocks. The setup will house two horses. On that hill above the stables is the Brackens' cottage. Wait until you see it all in the daylight, Katy. This is beautiful land."

Katy heard the enthusiasm in his voice and tried to ignore it. It wasn't easy because her own curiosity was getting the better of her. Until last night, she had been looking forward to living here. She had thought the place was going to be her home. Well, she reminded herself, it was still to be her home for the next three months.

"Looks like Bracken didn't leave any lights on in the main house. Dammit, I told him I wanted the porch light left on in case we got in after dark." Garrett slowed and finally stopped the car in a long, curving drive. He frowned at the darkened two-story house. The headlights picked up a small section of a wide, arched front door and a portion of rockery that enclosed a flower garden.

"Perhaps he forgot about the light," Katy suggested as she slowly opened her door and stepped out onto the drive. On the other side of the vehicle, Garrett's door slammed as he got out.

"Yeah, maybe he forgot," Garrett muttered as he searched for the house key. "Or maybe he started drinking too early in the afternoon."

"He's got an alcohol problem?"

"Atwood implied something of that nature. Didn't go into details. I'll talk to Bracken in the morning. If the man wants to stay on here, he's going to have to learn to follow orders."

Katy wisely said no more, but she privately hoped the unknown Emmett Bracken would learn quickly that his new employer allowed very little slack. As a teenager in her father's stables, he had always given Harry Randall his money's worth. Katy had learned during the past two months that Garrett had not changed in that respect. He worked hard and expected others to do the same.

The front door swung open on silent hinges as Garrett turned the key in the lock. He leaned inside and found the hall switch. An instant later light blazed, revealing a wide foyer with a floor of rich, burnished quarry tile. Katy stepped inside, smiling in spite of herself.

"Oh, this is lovely, Garrett," she whispered as she glanced around. The overhead light fixture, a handsome creation of wrought iron and glass, gleamed. Katy saw herself in an ornately framed mirror that hung above a long, polished table. She was vaguely startled by the woman who looked back at her. Her gray eyes seemed to dominate her face. They reflected a strange combination of caution and fatigue. Her hair was coming loose. Wispy tendrils curled around her nape. Her green blouse was rumpled from the hours she had spent sitting in the car. All in all, she did not look crisp, efficient or businesslike. Katy regretted that.

"I'm glad you like the house. I thought you would. I had you in mind when I told the designer what I wanted." Garrett's eyes were fastened on her as she wandered slowly through the foyer and into the living room.

Katy was deeply aware of Garrett's scrutiny as she turned on lamps and studied the warm glow of expansive hardwood floors. A massive stone fireplace dominated one wall. There was a collection of surprisingly beautiful leather furniture grouped around the fireplace. The large, fringed area rug on the floor was a modern interpretation of a Southwest Indian pattern. Floor-to-ceiling windows lined the wall that looked out over the darkened sea.

"The designer did a wonderful job," Katy admitted, looking around.

There was speculative satisfaction in Garrett's eyes. "I told her I wanted it perfect for my wife."

A twinge of guilt went through Katy as she realized just how much Garrett wanted her to like the place. Then she bracingly reminded herself that he had his own purely pragmatic, practical reasons for wanting her to be pleased. Her impulsive smile of pleasure faded.

"Kitchen's through there," Garrett said quickly as Katy turned around. "It's the old-fashioned type. Huge. Has everything in the way of appliances."

Katy walked through a dining room furnished with a long, elegant pine table and into a huge kitchen that had obviously been outfitted for someone who enjoyed cooking. The overhead light revealed acres of gleaming tile, professional cookware hanging from copper hooks and a round glass-topped kitchen table.

"During the past couple of months I found out you like to cook," Garrett murmured.

Katy glanced at him sharply. Apparently he had paid attention to some things of a personal nature during the past several weeks. She said nothing and opened the doors of the stainless steel refrigerator. The interior was empty.

"Good thing we picked up some groceries a while back," Garrett said briskly as he surveyed the empty shelves. "I'm starving."

Katy wondered if that was a hint that she was now supposed to assume her wifely chores. She shoved her hands into the pockets of her jeans and regarded her husband through thoughtful eyes. He looked as innocently expectant as it was possible for a man with Garrett's blunt, stark features to look.

Katy gave up the small battle before the first skirmish. She was hungry, too. This wasn't the time or place to draw lines. "Why don't you bring in the groceries and I'll see what I can do about dinner."

Garrett's mouth tilted in faintly concealed satisfaction. "Sounds like a good idea."

Forty-five minutes later Katy had put together a salad of tomatoes, cucumbers and feta cheese, rice and a simple shrimp curry. Garrett had spent the time unloading the car. He walked into the kitchen just as she was putting the food on the glass-topped table.

"It's been a long time since lunch," he announced. He sauntered over to the table and studied the neatly arranged salad and curry. He appeared to be pleased. "Smells good. Did you open the wine?"

"No." Katy watched him out of the corner of her eye as she finished the last of her preparations. "I didn't know if you would want a glass with dinner."

Garrett gave her a narrow look. "This is our first meal in our new home. It seems to me that warrants a glass of wine."

"Does it?" She hid her astonishment. It had never occurred to her that Garrett would concern himself with the small, intimate celebrations of life. "Well, given the circumstances of our marriage, I don't think we have to feel obliged to celebrate tonight." She sat down abruptly and reached for the salad bowl.

"This is a special event," Garrett said roughly, "and we are going to treat it with all due respect." He reached the refrigerator with two long, impatient strides and yanked open the door. He reached inside and withdrew the bottle of champagne Katy had last seen languishing in a warm ice bucket.

"I thought we left that behind at the hotel." She stared at Garrett as he took the bottle over to the counter and went to work on the cork.

"If it had been up to you, we would have left it behind. But since we paid through the teeth for that damned cotton-candy room, I thought we ought to get our money's worth out of it. The only thing salvageable this morning was the champagne, so I picked it up when we left." He threw Katy a glittering look and then went back to work on the cork.

Katy felt the warmth steal into her face. He didn't have to spell out the fact that he considered everything else about that infamous hotel room a total disaster. So did she. But it struck her as strange that he had packed the champagne. She hadn't given it a thought. She had just wanted to be free of the room and everything that had happened in it.

The cork came off with a contained explosion. None of the bubbling contents of the bottle was lost. It was typical of Garrett that he had maintained control over the champagne, Katy thought with a certain amount of resentment. He was always in control of everything.

Garrett saw her expression as he came back to the table with a couple of long-stemmed glasses he had found in a cupboard. "Are you going to remember our wedding night every time you drink champagne, honey?"

She did not like the soft, taunting edge in his voice. "Who knows? A couple of glasses of this stuff and I might even be able to forget all about our wedding night."

"Not a chance," he murmured as he sat down across from her and poured champagne. He put down the bottle, picked up a glass and handed it to her. Golden bubbles glinted between his fingers. Above the rim of the glass, golden eyes met Katy's. "It might not have been everything you wanted or expected in the way of a wedding night, but it *was* our wedding night, and the last thing I'm going to do is let you forget that fact."

Katy froze in the act of reaching across the small table to accept the glass of champagne. She sensed the force of his willpower reaching out to envelop her and she boldly tried to resist. "Some things are better off forgotten, Garrett."

"Some things," he corrected her, "get better with a little practice."

Katy drew a slow, steadying breath. She knew exactly what he was saying to her. He was telling her he fully expected to sleep with her.

"What we have is a business arrangement." Katy struggled to keep her voice neutral. She took the champagne from his hand and forced herself to take a sip. It struck her for the first time just what it meant to be totally alone with Garrett. She had spent very little time completely alone with him during the past two months, she realized. And on most of those few occasions, he had spent most of the time talking about his plans for the future. He had never focused on her the way he was doing tonight. It was, Katy discovered, unnerving to be the center of his complete, undivided attention. "You were the one who wanted that kind of arrangement, if you'll recall."

Garrett gave her a long look and then he took a swallow from his own glass. "I wasn't given much choice in the matter."

Katy stared at him pleadingly. "I don't think this is going to work, Garrett. I think we should cut our losses now, tonight, without trying to make a business arrangement out of what was meant to be a marriage."

"It's one thing for you to suggest we cut our losses," he retorted, putting down his champagne and picking up a fork. "You've got a lot less to lose than I do. Or so you've apparently concluded. But maybe you'll change your mind. Three months is a long time."

Three months was beginning to look like forever, Katy thought.

TWO HOURS LATER Katy climbed into bed. She glanced around the room just before switching off the bedside lamp. It was, she suspected, a guest bedroom, done in pleasant earth tones. This bedroom was smaller than the master suite down the hall, which Katy had discreetly left for the new master of the house.

As she curled up alone beneath the covers, she experienced a flash of resentment that mingled with a deep, underlying sadness. She didn't want to acknowledge the unhappiness, so she concentrated on the resentment. It was an emotion less likely to bring tears to her eyes.

Meanwhile, down the hall, the new master of the house emerged from the bathroom wearing only a pair of jeans and discovered what he had half expected to find. He was alone in the beautiful suite.

It was, Garrett knew, too much to hope that Katy would quietly acquiesce to sharing a bedroom for the next three months. But that hadn't stopped him from hoping, anyway. It would have made things so much easier. Somehow, Garrett told himself, if he could just persuade Katy to sleep with him on a normal basis, he knew he could gradually overcome her irrational reaction to the whole mess. Under ordinary circumstances she was such a sweet, soft, compliant creature. In addition, whether she wanted to acknowledge it or not, she was also a very sensual woman. Surely if he tapped into that sweetness and that softness and that sensuality over a long enough period of time he could convince her that what they had together was more than enough for both of them.

She had taken him by surprise with her unexpected flight into romantic fantasy land, but underneath it all she was still the realistic, gentle, undemanding woman he had come to know during the past couple of months. Once she'd looked up at him with the hero-worshiping eyes of a child. Last night he knew that expression of shy hero worship had been replaced with a woman's look of passion. Given time and propinquity, he was sure he could teach her to be contented with him.

Well, he had bought himself the time, but Katy seemed intent on denying him the element of propinquity where it counted most—in the bedroom.

Garrett stood in the middle of the room and eyed the closed door for a long moment, his brows in a rigid, determined line. Katy was just down the hall in one of the other three bedrooms. It was a cinch she wasn't going to come to him.

If anything was going to be done about the untenable situation, he would have to do it.

With a low oath, Garrett strode to the door, opened it and started down the long hall. He opened doors as he went along.

He found her in the last room and decided to take heart from the fact that the door wasn't locked. He twisted the knob and stepped inside. A startled movement from the bed drew his eyes instantly. In the shadows he could see her pale face and the deliciously tangled dark cloud of hair that framed her features. She looked very alone and very vulnerable in the double bed.

"Garrett!"

"Who were you expecting? The fairy-tale prince you thought you had married? Sorry, honey, you're stuck with the frog." He folded his arms and leaned one shoulder against the doorframe. He knew he was backlit by the hall light. All Katy could see of him was his silhouette. She wouldn't be able to read the expression on his face. Maybe that was just as well.

She propped herself up on her elbows, trying to see him more clearly. "Maybe it wasn't such a good idea for you to finish off the last of that champagne by yourself."

"I had to finish it off by myself. I didn't hear you offering to help. You quit after one glass."

"I didn't feel like drinking champagne."

"Why not?" he challenged, feeling put upon. "It's supposed to be so damned romantic." He'd salvaged that stupid bottle for her and she hadn't had more than half a glass. That fact had been annoying him all evening. Saving their wedding-night champagne had struck him as a brilliantly romantic move that morning when he'd first thought of it. Just the sort of move that would appeal to the new, unexpected and unpredictable side of Katy that he was discovering.

"Garrett, please. The only way we're going to get through the next three months together is if you make some effort to be civil."

"A man can't be civil all the time."

"You can," she retorted. "You've been perfectly civil to me since I met you. At least, you were perfectly civil until . . ."

"Never mind, I don't want to hear about the exact moment when you began to realize that I wasn't your knight in shining armor. I already know the big revelation struck you when I demonstrated that I was fully capable of making love to you without giving you a mushy, meaningless declaration of undying love."

"That's enough, Garrett." Her voice was quiet but laced with stubbornness. "More than enough. I don't have to listen to any more of this."

"The hell you don't. You're my *wife*."

"I'm your employee," she shot back. "Now close the door and go back to your own room before I charge you with sexual harassment." She lay back down, turned her face toward the wall and pulled the quilt up over her shoulder.

Garrett stared at the curve of her shoulder and decided he now knew how the expression "cold shoulder" had originated. He wondered if the man who had first coined it had ever figured out a way of thawing out a frozen wife. If so, he had not been generous enough to pass along the information to posterity. Every man, it seemed, was fated to have to discover the trick on his own.

"Just tell me one thing, Katy."

"What do you want to know?"

"I want you to tell me if I was really such a clumsy lover last night that now you can't stand the thought of me touching you."

There was a fraught silence from the bed before Katy said stiffly, "You know the answer to that."

"No, I don't know the answer. If I did, I wouldn't be asking."

"For heaven's sake, Garrett."

*"Just tell me the truth."*

"All right," she stormed, pulling the covers up over her head, "I'll tell you the truth. As far as the physical side of things went, everything was...was perfect. There. Are you satisfied? I have no complaints in that department. Now get out of here."

Garrett started to back quietly out of the bedroom. He stopped when he saw Katy lower the covers to her chin. She glared at him in the shadows.

"Garrett?"

Hope soared in him. "What is it, honey?"

"Was she very beautiful?"

He looked at her blankly. "Was who very beautiful?"

"That woman you thought you loved all those years ago."

Hope turned into exasperation. "That's a damned fool question, Katy, I don't even remember what she looked like. I said I learned a lesson from her, I didn't say I carried her picture around in my wallet."

"I just wondered."

"You mean you wondered if I was carrying a torch for her," he snapped, thoroughly irritated. "The answer is no."

"But how do you know?" Katy persisted.

"Because five years ago I ran into her again," Garrett said, feeling goaded. "I could have had her then. Instead I took one look at her and thanked my lucky stars I'd escaped the first time. She was one cold, calculating little bitch. Satisfied?"

"I guess so."

"You'd better be. The subject is now closed." Garrett swung away from the door and stalked back the hall to his lonely room. His body was painfully taut with unreleased desire. He took one look at the empty bed waiting for him and then went on into the bathroom to acquaint himself with the therapeutic effects of a cold shower.

# 5

KATY WAS in the middle of grilling corn cakes the next morning when the knock sounded on the kitchen door. She had told herself during the long, restless night that she would feed Garrett cold cereal for breakfast or maybe even leave him to fend for himself. But somehow she couldn't bring herself to do it.

It was undoubtedly some bizarre form of wifely guilt that was prompting her, she decided in irritation. She was going to have to learn how to overcome that. Perhaps she should learn how to concentrate more on her newfound temper. There was something liberating about discovering one had a temper.

Startled by the knock, she hastily flicked the last corn cake off the griddle and onto a warming plate. Then she headed for the door. She wondered if she should call Garrett. He was still in the shower as far as she knew. He seemed to have taken a lot of showers in the past twenty-four hours.

Katy opened the door to find a wiry, withered man on the step. The man could have been anywhere between fifty and seventy. It was hard to tell because a lifetime of outdoor work had marked him with a deep tan and a network of sun-induced lines on his lean face. He was wearing an ancient pair of jeans, worn boots, a faded plaid shirt and a battered cap. He tipped the brim of the cap briefly and studied her with rheumy blue eyes that were as faded as his shirt. Years of drinking had left their mark, but he was obviously not drunk this morning.

"Morning, ma'am. I'm Emmett Bracken. You must be Mrs. Coltrane. Coltrane said he was going to bring a wife back with him."

"How do you do?" She decided not to clarify her exact status in the household. It was too hard to explain, especially while she was wearing a wedding ring. She made a mental note to remember to remove the ring later. "It's nice to meet you, Emmett. I understand you've been holding things together around here since the owner more or less abandoned the place a couple of years ago."

"Never thought I'd see the day anyone except an Atwood lived on this hill. Could have knocked me and my wife over with a feather the day we heard the place had been sold. Been real sad watching Atwood get rid of the land bit by bit these past few years. We thought he'd stay here till he died. Who'd have thought he'd up and move to Palm Springs?"

"Yes, well, I'm sure it was a surprise to a lot of local people," Katy said diplomatically.

"You can say that again," Bracken said in his slow drawl. "Royce Hutton had himself a real fit when he found out the house and this last piece of property was going to a new owner."

"Royce Hutton?"

"Yeah, owns a few acres on down the road. Breeds fancy cattle. Sells his stock all over the world to folks trying to improve their breeding programs. He's had his eye on this piece of land for years. Tried for the past couple of years to get Atwood to sell to him, but Atwood got real stubborn. Hutton was with Atwood's boy the night young Brent died. Atwood never wanted anything to do with Hutton after that. Didn't want anything to do with any of the kids who were involved that night."

"I see," Katy said, vaguely remembering Garrett's telling her the story. She wished Garrett would appear. She wasn't quite sure what to say to Emmett Bracken. "Won't you come in for coffee, Emmett?"

"No thanks. Just had some of my wife's coffee. It'll hold me. I stopped by because Coltrane told me he'd want to start work early on those stables. Says he's bringing his horse here in a few days."

"I'm sure he will want to get to work early, but he hasn't had a chance to eat breakfast yet. He'll be out as soon as he's finished."

Bracken nodded, accepting that. "Okay. Tell him I'll be in the stables."

"I'll tell him."

Bracken hesitated, glancing past her into the kitchen. "This place has sure been changed around. Doesn't even look like the same house. Sure seems strange not having any Atwoods here." He shook his head. "After all these years. Me and the missus were sure the boy would take over one day."

"I can understand that."

"He had a thing going with my daughter, Felice, you know." There was a touch of pride in the man's voice.

Katy cleared her throat. "No, I didn't know."

"My Felice is a real beauty. They were gonna get married. She and Brent were seein' each other real regular. Then the accident happened. Everything sort of fell apart after that. Silas's wife died and gradually Silas just seemed to lose interest in the place. My wife took it hard. Never quite got over it. Had her heart set on Felice marrying young Brent."

"Life doesn't always go as planned," Katy said, feeling very wise from recent experience.

"No, it sure don't."

"What happened to your daughter?" Katy couldn't resist asking.

"She went off to college and got herself a job workin' for a big company that makes things like stereos and those gadgets that let you record TV shows. She seems happy enough. It's the missus who never quite forgot what might have happened if young Brent hadn't gone and broke his neck that night." Bracken tipped his old hat again. "Well, see you later, Mrs. Coltrane. My wife'll be by in a while to say hello. Tell your man I'm getting started."

"I will," Katy promised. She closed the door slowly, sensing Garrett's presence behind her.

"Was that Bracken?" Garrett asked crisply as he strode into the kitchen. He was rolling back the cuffs of his long-sleeved blue work shirt. There was a faint frown of concentration on his face as he attended to the small task.

"Yes." Katy stood looking at him, both hands behind her on the doorknob. She felt a flash of wistfulness. As she had told Emmett Bracken, life didn't always go as planned. This was her first morning in her new home. Things should have been different. "He said to tell you he'll be starting work in the stables."

Garrett nodded perfunctorily. "Good. What's for breakfast?" He glanced toward the stove.

"Corn cakes and maple syrup. The coffee's ready." Instantly she made herself sound more brisk. Dammit, she could be as efficient and businesslike as he was. It had been her idea in the first place to be efficient and businesslike. Katy launched herself away from the door and aimed for the stove. "Sit down and I'll get you a cup. Emmett was just telling me about Royce Hutton wanting this house and the land around it."

"Hutton will learn to live with the disappointment of not getting what he wanted," Garrett said laconically. "We all have to learn that lesson sooner or later, don't we?"

Katy wondered if there was a message in that remark intended for her. She carried the hot platter of corn cakes over to the table. "Yes, we all have to learn that." She sat down. "When do you think you'll have the stall and paddock ready for Red Dazzle?"

"Not long. A couple of days' work should get one of the stalls in order. I'll arrange for a hay and grain delivery as soon as possible."

Katy nodded, determined to maintain the businesslike atmosphere that seemed to have established itself. "Mrs. Bracken is coming by later this morning to go through the house with me."

"Fine," Garrett murmured coolly. There was a pause as he bit into the corn cakes. "Sure am glad you can cook," he finally said with grudging appreciation. "Bracken's wife can take care of the house during the day, but I'd just as soon have you doing the cooking. I don't like having people underfoot first thing in the morning or during dinner. I like my privacy."

"Does that mean I should add cooking to my new job description?" Katy tried to speak lightly, but she knew there was a sting in the words.

Garrett slanted her a chilling look. "You've got my reasons for marrying you all figured out, don't you?"

"I figured them out a little late, but, yes, I finally did figure them out."

Garrett forked up another bite of corn cakes. "You are one stubborn female. I don't know why I didn't see that before I married you."

"Maybe you didn't see it because you weren't really looking at me," Katy said quietly. "All you saw were the trappings that surrounded me. Good social connections, a good pedigree, a useful education. All the things you lacked while you were growing up. On top of everything else I seemed good-natured, undemanding and biddable. What more could a man want in a wife?"

Garrett looked at her, amber eyes glinting with an emotion that might have been anger, annoyance or warning. "Do you really want me to answer that?"

Katy flushed and speared a piece of corn cake. "No."

"I didn't think so. Katy, things are tense enough between us. For both our sakes, I suggest you don't spend a lot of time baiting me."

Katy wasn't certain how to take that so she kept quiet.

To her surprise, matters seemed to stabilize during the next two days. She went out of her way to be polite and businesslike when she was with Garrett, and he reciprocated with a remote civility that didn't quite mask his dissatisfaction. Katy got the feeling he was determined to give the situation time. She thought about telling him that time wasn't going to make any difference but thought better of it. He was right—baiting him might be a dangerous pastime.

Nadine Bracken, a dour-faced woman who appeared to be in the same age range as her husband proved helpful, if not particularly talkative. When Katy praised her for taking such excellent care of the main house she just shrugged.

"Been takin' care of this house for as long as I can remember. I've always had a feeling for this place," she had said. "I went to work for the Atwoods when I was in high school. Emmett did, too. The Atwoods always made us feel like we were family, if you know what I mean. I even thought we might be family, one day." She'd favored Katy with a strange look. "Emmett and I thought our girl, Felice, would wind up livin' here in this house."

Katy hadn't quite known what to say to that, so she'd changed the subject. "I gather the interior designer Garrett hired made several changes."

Nadine had stared balefully at the new furniture in the living room. "She did. Acted as if no one important had ever lived here. Had no respect. Just came through and tore the place up from one end to the other."

"It looks lovely now," Katy had said, feeling an odd need to defend Garrett's choice of interior designers. Garrett had given the orders to redo the place because he had wanted to please his new wife. Katy felt a familiar twinge of emotion at the thought. She was going to have to try harder to avoid those guilt pangs.

ROYCE HUTTON dropped by to introduce himself on Katy's third morning in her new home. Garrett was out taking a look at the final preparations for Red Dazzle at the time, and it was Katy who answered the door to find a tall, rangy, good-looking man in his late thirties on the doorstep. His grin was infectious.

"You must be the new Mrs. Coltrane. I'm your neighbor, Royce Hutton. Came by to introduce myself properly and then kick myself one more time around the block for missing out on this piece of property. Hope you're enjoying your new home."

Katy was unable to resist the humor in Royce Hutton's hazel eyes. After the tension of living with Garrett's grim, remote mood, she found it was a relief to speak to someone who was obviously intent on being charming. "Please come in, Royce. I heard you wanted the house and land. It is a beautiful setting, isn't it?"

"You can say that again." Royce followed her into the living room, his eyes sweeping over the furnishings. "Hey, Coltrane really went first-class in here, didn't he? I heard he spent a fortune having this place redone. Looks like something out of a magazine."

"Yes, it does, doesn't it? Garrett wanted it to be polished and perfect. Can I offer you a cup of coffee?"

"Sounds great."

Nadine Bracken materialized silently behind them, wiping her hands on a dish towel. "I'll get the coffee, Mrs. Coltrane."

Katy smiled gratefully. "Thanks, Nadine."

Royce raised an eyebrow as the unsmiling woman disappeared. "The Brackens have been here forever, you know," he murmured. "They took it hard when old

Silas got rid of the place. Is Garrett going to keep them on?"

"As far as I know," Katy said carefully. "Garrett hasn't said anything one way or the other, but things seem to be working out. Please sit down."

"Thanks." Royce threw himself casually into a white leather chair. The action revealed the fine tooling on a pair of handmade boots. "Heard your last name was Randall up until a couple of days ago and that your people breed Arabians. Would that be the Randall Stud Farm people?"

"News travels, doesn't it?"

Royce chuckled. "Coltrane didn't go out of his way to keep it a secret. I got the impression he was very proud to be bringing you home as his wife."

Proud to be bringing a *Randall* home for a wife, Katy thought. That sounded like Garrett. She was saved from having to make a response by the appearance of Mrs. Bracken. "Oh, here's the coffee. Thanks, Nadine."

Nadine nodded once, saying nothing, set down the tray and disappeared again. Katy began to pour.

"I did some business with your father a while back," Royce continued easily as he accepted his cup. "Sent one of my best mares down to Randall Farm to be bred to Silver Moon. Got a terrific little colt out of it."

"What was the mare's name?"

"Morning Mist."

Katy smiled. "I remember her. I was managing my father's breeding operation until recently. Silver Moon is a beautiful stallion. His offspring always get his intelligence as well as his conformation. You'll win some championships with that colt."

Royce grinned. "Guess I should have come along with the mare. I could have met you before Coltrane did."

A boot step sounded on the polished wood floor, and Garrett's voice cut into the conversation with the lethal swiftness of a razor blade.

"It wouldn't have done you any good to meet Katy a year ago, Hutton. You were married at the time." Garrett strode into the room, his eyes skimming briefly over his wife and settling on Royce Hutton.

"Just another example of my bad timing," Royce said dryly.

"Win some, lose some." Garrett sat down on the couch beside Katy. He seemed totally unconcerned about the possibility of transferring the dust from his jeans to the immaculate leather. He was apparently far more concerned about staking a quiet claim on Katy. "Any coffee left?"

"I'll have Nadine bring another cup." Katy began to grow uneasy as she quietly arranged for the coffee. Garrett was radiating a new variety of tension, a version she had never before detected in him. For an instant she wondered if it was jealousy, then she told herself it was more likely a form of possessiveness. As she surreptitiously studied her husband's hard face, it occurred to her that he was the kind of man who had learned the hard way how to hang on to what he considered his, even if the possession in question did not care to be possessed.

Royce Hutton's easygoing manner defused the potentially awkward situation. He seemed willing enough to respect Garrett's obvious claim to both the house and the woman. Katy wasn't sure she liked being written off as another man's property, but she was grateful there wasn't going to be a scene.

"I didn't drop by just to introduce myself and allow Coltrane here to gloat." Royce smiled at Katy a few minutes later as he finished his coffee. "I wanted to invite you both over for a few drinks with the neighbors this evening. I know it's short notice, but I figured what with you two being on your honeymoon, you probably weren't booked solid with social engagements."

"I'd love to meet the neighbors," Katy said quickly, even as Garrett's heavy dark brows came together over his narrowed eyes. She was not certain if she was accepting because she didn't want to face another long evening alone with her husband or if she was subtly and only half-consciously trying to challenge him in some way. There were moments lately when she didn't understand herself.

Garrett gave her a slow, speculative glance, but he finally nodded without much enthusiasm. "We'll be there," he said calmly to Royce Hutton.

"Mission accomplished," Royce announced, getting to his feet. "I'd better be on my way. I've got some Australians arriving this afternoon to look at my Charolais-Angus crosses."

"Thanks for dropping by," Katy said warmly as she opened the front door. "Garrett and I will be looking forward to this evening."

"Right. See you later." Royce walked out to his BMW, climbed inside, turned the key and backed out of the driveway.

"You don't have to stand in the doorway staring after him," Garrett muttered.

Katy blinked in surprise at the harsh tone. "I wasn't staring after him."

"I hope not. I wouldn't want you getting any ideas about Hutton. And I sure as hell don't want him getting any ideas about you."

Katy's eyes widened. "That's not likely," she retorted.

"Think not? The man's only been divorced a few months. He's out to prove he's still got what it takes. Lately he's been chasing anything shaped like a female."

"Garrett, you're being ridiculous."

"I'm being careful."

"I don't know what you're so upset about," Katy said through her teeth. She was suddenly furious. "After all, Royce knew all about my father's farm. He knew I was Harry Randall's daughter, and I'm certain he'll make sure everyone at the cocktail party tonight also knows who I am. That's one of the reasons you married me, wasn't it? So that you could get some mileage out of my family connections? You wanted to prove to yourself and everyone else that you were rich enough and successful enough now to marry the daughter of the man whose stables you had once cleaned. Thanks to Royce's invitation you'll be able to show off your new acquisition this evening."

Something sharp and violent flared in Garrett's eyes. "You don't know what the hell you're saying."

"I'm only saying what several other people were saying at the wedding."

He stared at her. "And you believed it?"

"Not then. I didn't believe it until later when I realized you didn't love me. Then I had to look for other reasons why you married me. The fact that I was Harry Randall's daughter explained a lot of your interest in me. I was too stupid to look for the real reasons for our marriage before I found myself walking down the aisle."

"Dammit, Katy, the only thing you've been looking for lately is trouble, and if you're not careful, you're going to find it. I did not marry you just to prove to the world that I was now in the position to marry my former employer's daughter. For God's sake, use your head. Do you honestly think I'd tie myself to a woman I didn't want just to prove I could marry her? I'm not a masochist."

The sound of a truck engine out in the driveway halted Garrett. Grateful for the diversion, Katy glanced through the open door. A truck pulling a horse trailer was approaching.

"I think Red Dazzle is here," Katy said stiffly.

Garrett shoved his hat down low over his eyes and stepped outside. "About time." He walked away with long, impatient strides, heading toward the truck and trailer.

Katy stood in the doorway wishing she had kept her mouth shut. She didn't move until a faint tingle down her spine told her she was not alone. She swung around a little nervously and saw Nadine Bracken standing in the arched doorway that opened onto the dining room. The woman was just standing there, staring. Katy wondered how much she had overheard.

"You gave me a start," Katy said, summoning a smile.

"I just wondered if you wanted me to change the beds."

Katy winced at the realization that Nadine Bracken knew her new employers were not sleeping together.

"No, that can wait until tomorrow. You can go now. I think everything's under control for today. Garrett and I are going out this evening."

"All right." Nadine moved soundlessly out of sight.

Katy turned back to watch the scene outside the door. Garrett was deep in conversation with the young driver of the truck. Katy walked outside and slowly strolled toward the horse trailer. She was curious about Red Dazzle. Memories of a stolen day at the county fair rodeo when she was fifteen drifted through her head. She'd had eyes only for Garrett that day, but she did have a vague recollection of a sleepy-looking chestnut quarter horse built like a bulldog. She also remembered the way that same lethargic-looking creature had exploded out of a chute in hot pursuit of a calf. The memory made Katy smile. Garrett had won big that day.

Red Dazzle must be getting on in years, Katy realized. The gelding was probably seventeen or eighteen by now. That was old age for a horse. It said something about Garrett that he had taken care of Red Dazzle all these years after leaving the rodeo circuit. Something softened within Katy as she thought about that.

Red Dazzle was in the process of being unloaded from the trailer by the time Katy reached the vehicle. Katy smiled slightly as she watched the animal back down the ramp. Garrett was at the horse's head, guiding him. It was clear Red Dazzle did not need any assistance. This business of being untrailered was an old routine for him. The horse made a soft, woofling sound against Garrett's hand by way of greeting. Then he absently swished his tail. He looked patiently bored.

"He doesn't look any more wide awake now than he did the last time I saw him," Katy said, wanting to break the new barrier of unpleasantness she had just succeeded in erecting between herself and her husband. She wished she'd had the sense to control her tongue a few minutes earlier.

Garrett glanced at her, as if trying to identify the unexpected note of friendliness in her voice. Red Dazzle's ears twitched at the sound of her voice, and he turned his large head to give the stranger a sleepy-eyed glance.

"Old Red here looked this way the day he was born. Dozed off about five minutes after he'd finally got up on his feet for the first time, and he's been busy conserving his energy ever since. He's not like those high strung Arabians your father raises, all nerves and delicate breeding."

Katy had the impression the comment about nerves and delicate breeding was meant to include her as well as her father's horses. "No," she agreed smoothly, "there's nothing delicate about Red Dazzle." Or about his owner, she added silently.

Garrett stroked the dark chestnut neck with brusque affection. But his expression was curious as he looked at Katy. "When did you see Red before today?"

"At a fair rodeo when I was fifteen. I snuck away from school because I'd heard you—" Katy bit off the revealing confession. She tried to cover it with a shrug. "Some friends and I decided to skip school and go to the rodeo at the county fair. It seemed exciting at the time. I had never cut school in my life. A big event for me. You and Red Dazzle were riding, as I recall."

"Is that right?" Garrett spoke reflectively, but there was an alert gleam in his golden eyes. "What was the attraction? I thought you were into fancy hunting and performance classes in those days. Itsy-bitsy English saddles, little nipped-in jackets, riding breeches and knee-high boots." A trace of humor crept into his voice. "Why would you want to go to a dusty, dirty rodeo and watch a bunch of guys in old jeans take a lot of falls in the mud?"

Katy's chin came up. Damned if she was going to let him goad her like this. "It made a change of pace."

"I'll just bet it did. Did you enjoy watching me fall in the mud?"

Katy bit her lip and then admitted in a soft rush, "It occurred to me at the time that you'd eventually break every bone in your body if you kept on with the rodeo circuit."

"You were right. It's a young man's game. No future in it. That's why I got out of it when I did." Garrett stared at her, his hand still moving idly over Red Dazzle's neck. "Did you think I'd broken a few bones that day?"

"Yes." Her voice was stark as she recalled the tremor of fear that had gone through her when she'd watched him come out of the chute on top of a huge bull. Garrett had hung on for a high-scoring ride, but when he'd finally hit the dirt the bull had turned on him. Things had been close for a while. Garrett had dodged horns and the crowd had roared its approval until the bull had been distracted. Katy had been shaking in her seat by the time the whole thing was over. A short time later Garrett was scoring points in the calf-roping competition just as if he hadn't been facing death or serious injury half an hour earlier.

"But as it turns out you were the one who eventually got hurt so badly you couldn't bring yourself to ride again," Garrett pointed out quietly.

"Life has its little ironies, doesn't it?" Katy started to turn away.

"Katy."

Unwillingly she halted and glanced back at Garrett. "What is it?"

"That day you skipped school to go to the rodeo . . ."

"What about it?"

"Did you do it just to see me ride?" Garrett asked softly.

He knew, she thought. He'd noticed her small slip earlier and he'd put two and two together. She tried for a serenely haughty smile. "That was a long time ago, Garrett. I've forgotten now exactly why I thought going to the rodeo was worth the risk of skipping school." Katy headed determinedly toward the house.

Garrett watched her go, silently appreciating the curve of her derriere which was very nicely outlined by her jeans. He could still remember the feel of that particular curve and the memory produced an uncomfortably strained sensation in the front of his own jeans. A side glance at the driver of the truck showed that Garrett wasn't the only one enjoying the scenery. It seemed to Garrett that every man in the vicinity was eyeing his wife today. First Royce Hutton and now the young man standing nearby.

"I'm going to put Red in his stall," Garrett said roughly. There was enough of an edge to his voice to capture the younger man's attention. "I'll be back in a few minutes."

"Sure," the young man said. There was a faint flush under his tan. "I can wait."

Red Dazzle woofled again and experimentally lipped the sleeve of Garrett's shirt.

Garrett tugged gently on the gelding's halter. "Let's go, pal. You know something? She was lying. I could see it in her eyes. She has a terrible time when it comes to lying. The truth is, she skipped school that day just so she could watch you and me be heroes for a few minutes. I do believe we were the objects of a teenage crush. Her parents would have flipped in those days if they'd known their daughter had stars in her eyes for a low-class, blue-collar rodeo cowboy who was sure-fired guaranteed never going to amount to anything."

Red Dazzle sighed gustily, but it was difficult to tell if he was responding to the remark or simply expressing mild boredom. Garrett led him toward the roomy stall and paddock that had been prepared.

"You know, Red, back in our glory days, you used to be able to make me look real good in front of a crowd," Garrett told the horse as he opened the stall door. "Too bad I can't just climb on board and look like a knight in shining armor again."

Red Dazzle wasn't paying any attention. He had spotted the hay in the corner of his new stall. He bestirred himself into a slightly speedier pace and entered his new home. Garrett closed the door and was in the process of securing it carefully when Emmett Bracken walked into the stable.

"So that's the critter we've been waiting for, huh?" Emmett shoved his hat back on his head and surveyed Red Dazzle's large, muscular rear quarters.

"That's him." Garrett leaned on the stall door. "You know, Emmett, I think it's time I started looking for a good-tempered little mare for my wife."

"She ride?" Emmett asked.

"She got hurt a few years back and hasn't ridden since. Got spooked. But I think it's time she got back in the saddle."

"What does she think about the idea?" Emmett asked. "Folks that get spooked by a horse often don't want to get back on one." There was clear skepticism in his faded eyes. "And the more time that passes, the less they want to try."

"Now, Emmett, you know better than to ask a woman for her opinion. Especially when it's a subject she's already made up her mind about."

"Meaning she isn't going to think much of the idea of getting back in the saddle," Emmett concluded.

"We'll see," Garrett said.

He left Red Dazzle in the stall and went to talk to the man who had transported the horse to his new home. The more he thought about getting Katy back into the saddle, the more Garrett liked the idea. Riding would establish a bond between himself and his wife, he decided. It was something the two of them could do together. It would be one more thing they had in common.

In addition, he told himself, Katy was bound to feel some sense of gratitude toward him if he helped her overcome the traumatic fear that had plagued her since that barn fire. A man could do a lot with a woman's gratitude.

He might even be able to turn it back into love.

## 6

SEVERAL HOURS LATER Garrett stood quietly near a door that opened onto a patio at Royce Hutton's home. The evening was warm, but there was a storm moving in from the sea. It would reach the coast soon. Garrett glanced at his watch and decided he and Katy would probably wind up driving home in the rain.

Hutton had gathered most of the neighborhood for his informal cocktail party. The people filling his living room were casually dressed, but there was no mistaking the fact that they were a successful, affluent group. Garrett recognized many of them. There were a couple of professors from the nearby college, as well as a variety of other people ranging from software entrepreneurs to wine makers. Several of those present considered themselves gentleman farmers with strong interests in Thoroughbreds, pedigrees and expensive stallions.

It was a collection of people, Garrett knew, who wouldn't have given him a second glance ten years ago, but today they accepted him as their equal. They also accepted his wife. Her background allowed her to slip right into the community, just as he had known it would.

That thought brought back memories of the accusation Katy had made that afternoon. Dammit, he hadn't married her to gain an entrée into this world. The image of her accusing eyes made him set his back teeth. He had known she was a soft, gentle little thing, but her vulnerability surprised him. Just because he hadn't re-assured her with a melodramatic declaration of undying love, she had jumped to a whole truckload of wrong-headed conclusions.

As he listened to the cheerful chatter around him, Garrett sipped a beer and watched his wife deal gracefully with a talkative older man who was deep into a discussion about bloodlines. Katy was at ease with the topic, and she was obviously charming her new acquaintance as well as impressing him with the extent of her knowledge on the subject. Her eyes were alive with interest, and her smile was enough to make Garrett want to throw her over his shoulder and carry her off to the nearest bed. Now that he knew about the blazing sensuality hidden deep within her, he couldn't stop himself from dwelling on his condition of enforced celibacy. Three long months of temptation and an aching need loomed ahead of him. It made him groan to think of all the time he had wasted before the wedding.

On the other hand, Garrett thought gloomily, if he'd taken Katy to bed before the wedding she might have made her devastating "discovery" that much sooner and canceled the marriage plans. At least this way he had a tenuous hold on her for three months.

The only problem was that it was going to drive him crazy holding on to something he couldn't have.

Then he remembered the look in her eyes when she had confessed to the skipped day of school all those years ago. She'd had a crush on him back then—there was no doubt about it. And two months ago when he had come back into her life, she had convinced herself she was in love with him. On their wedding night she had given herself to him wholeheartedly.

Surely that kind of emotion didn't just dry up and disappear in a matter of hours, even if he had botched the wedding night. Garrett studied the disintegrating foam in his glass as his mind worked through the problem. He needed to find a way past the barriers she had erected between them. He wished he knew as much about romancing a woman as he did about handling a horse or terrorizing a banker who was threatening to foreclose on a Coltrane and Company client.

"So how's married life, Coltrane?"

Garrett inclined his head briefly at the sound of the familiar masculine voice, but he kept his eyes on Katy. "Interesting, Dan."

Dan Barton, a neatly dressed, well-groomed man about Garrett's age, grinned. His gaze followed Garrett's. "I can see you're still in the adjustment stage."

"What stage is that?"

"The stage where you're discovering you can't always tell what she's thinking. Women are strange creatures, my friend. Fascinating but strange."

"I'll buy that." Garrett took another sip of his beer. He liked Dan. He had met him when the two of them had been invited to do some guest lectures for some college extension courses. Dan was an accountant. His talk on farming finances had neatly dovetailed with Garrett's discussion of farm management. Since that first set of classes, he and Dan had frequently appeared together in similar situations.

"Glad to see you had the sense to pick a lady who knows something about your business. I talked to her earlier. She's an expert in her own right, isn't she?"

"Her family has been breeding Arabian show horses since before she was born," Garrett said. "She won a hell of a lot of ribbons when she was younger. Katy has been managing her father's stud farm for the past couple of years."

"She'll be an asset to your consulting business."

"I thought so," Garrett responded moodily.

"Sounds like a perfect marriage to me."

"It's going to be," Garrett vowed quietly. Then he noticed Royce Hutton making his way through the crowd toward Katy. Garrett moved away from the wall. "Excuse me, Dan. I'd better be getting back to my wife."

Dan's eyebrows rose as he gave Garrett a knowing look. "I understand completely. Hutton's been on the prowl lately. A divorce will do that to a man. Makes him act a little crazy for a while."

Katy saw Garrett approaching at the same moment she noticed Royce Hutton making his way toward her. She wondered if it was coincidence or if Garrett was just feeling possessive and protective. Deciding to think positive, she greeted her husband with a demure smile. When he put his hand around her waist she made no effort to pull away. Hutton reached her side a moment later and stood grinning down at her.

"Looks like Coltrane still remembers a few tricks from his rodeo days. He's got you on a short rope, Katy."

Katy flushed as several people nearby laughed. She felt Garrett's hand tighten at her waist and looked up to find him regarding her with a faint smile. His eyes were gleaming.

"We live in a dangerous age," Garrett said blandly. "A man has to take care of his valuables." He glanced at his watch. "I think it's about time we headed for home, honey," he said to Katy.

"There speaks the newly married man," someone remarked with a chuckle. "Can't wait to get home after a party."

"I remember those days well," another man said with a theatrical sigh. His wife poked him. There was a round of good-natured comments and best wishes for the newlyweds.

Katy felt an uncomfortable warmth spread up into her cheeks. She thought about the two separate beds waiting at home. This sort of teasing would have been bad enough if the marriage had been for real. Given her present state of détente with Garrett, however, it was almost unbearable. She wanted nothing more than to escape. When Garrett applied a little mild pressure in the direction of the door she went with him willingly.

"Good night, Royce. Thank you for having us over. It was a pleasure to meet everyone." Katy spoke quickly, trying to get the formalities concluded before Garrett had whisked her out the door.

"My pleasure, Katy." Royce grinned wickedly. "We'll see you again soon."

The rain was coming down in sheets as the door closed behind Garrett and Katy. Lightning crackled in the distance.

"Stay here," Garrett ordered, depositing Katy beneath the shelter of the porch. "I'll get the car."

"It's not that far away," Katy protested. "We can both make a dash for it."

"Dammit, Katy, I said, stay where you are. There's no need for both of us to get soaked. I'll be right back." He left her on the top step and moved out into the rain.

Katy stifled a sigh and stayed where she was. So much for trying to be helpful. The last thing she wanted to be was a nuisance. Garrett had married a *partner*, she reminded herself. She was determined to act like one.

But he seemed determined to treat her like a wife.

The unbidden thought danced through her head, creating all sorts of wistful, hopeful feelings. She had been contending with those treacherous feelings for three days now, and she didn't know how much longer she could push them aside.

The truth was, she was very much in love with her husband and she was woman enough to know he wanted her. On top of that, they were living under the same roof. That combination of emotions and circumstances was enough to undermine even the most stubbornly held decision. Only the heat of her recently discovered temper had kept her going this long. Katy was astute enough to recognize that she wouldn't be able to rely on it much longer. Living in a state of high dudgeon was totally alien to her nature.

Katy gazed out through the pouring rain and saw her immediate future with devastating clarity. She was never going to make it through three months playing the role of Garrett's business associate and roommate when the role she longed to play was that of wife.

She was still dealing with that realization when the lights of the white Mercedes sliced through the rain. A few seconds later the vehicle was in front of her and the passenger door was being thrust open.

"Hurry, Katy, or you'll get drenched."

Katy went down the steps as quickly as she dared. The last thing she wanted to endure was a fall in the mud caused by her weak ankle.

But she made it safely into the dry warmth of the car with only a few splashes of rain on her coat.

This storm certainly came in quickly," she said, striving for a neutral comment as she buckled her seat belt.

"Yeah."

So much for neutral conversation. Silence descended inside the car. It was similar to the silence that had accompanied the drive from Garrett's home to Hutton's earlier that evening.

Well, there was no denying the drive back was going to require a great deal of concentration on Garrett's part. The rain was descending in torrents, obscuring the road a few feet ahead. Minutes passed.

"Did you enjoy yourself?" Garrett finally asked.

"It was a pleasant evening."

There was another tense pause, and then Garrett said coolly, "I've met most of those people at one time or another during the past few years while I've been building up the consulting business."

"So I gathered." Katy wondered what he was trying to say. She sensed there was a message hidden somewhere in the words. "They seem nice, for the most part."

Garrett shrugged. "They are. Hutton's running a little wild these days because of the divorce, and a few of the others have a tendency to think the official poverty line is anything below an income of a hundred thousand a year, but they're decent people."

"I believe you." She still felt she was missing something. Apparently Garrett did, too, because the next time he spoke, his low, rough voice sounded almost explosive.

"Katy, I've been accepted by that crowd for the past five years. I didn't need your family name to get them to issue invitations. All I needed was an income level equivalent to theirs and the ability to talk their language."

Katy sucked in her breath. So that was it. He was trying to prove he hadn't married her just because she was a Randall. In the darkness Katy studied her folded hands. "I'm sorry about what I said this afternoon, Garrett. I had no right to accuse you of marrying me just to use my family connections."

"You may not like all the reasons I had for marrying you, but I want it clear that I never had any intention of using you as bait to attract important clients or to get myself into certain social circles."

She knew then just how deeply she had offended him. Her hands twisted together. "I know that, Garrett. You're much too proud to use a woman in that way. I was angry this afternoon. Angry and upset. Both of us have been under a lot of stress during the past few days."

"Unnecessary stress," Garrett said bluntly.

"We're living in a very difficult situation," Katy said carefully.

"We're living in a damned unnatural situation. A stupid situation. A crazy mixed-up totally idiotic situation. It's enough to drive a sane man over the edge."

Katy studied him with a sidelong glance. Garrett's face was set in stern lines. His hands gripped the wheel so tightly that she thought he might crack it.

"It isn't going to work, is it, Garrett?" Katy finally asked in a very quiet voice.

"What isn't going to work? Three months of living together like buddies who are sharing an apartment? No, it isn't going to work."

Katy drew a deep breath. She had to make a decision. She couldn't go on like this and neither could Garrett.

"Perhaps," Katy began with exquisite caution, "perhaps we could try again. If you want to, that is."

"*Katy.*" Garrett sounded stunned.

"Maybe you're right," she said slowly, trying to sort out the thoughts that had been plaguing her for the past few days. "Maybe I went into this looking for the wrong things. Maybe I did expect too much. I let myself get tangled up in a lot of old, juvenile emotions that I should have discarded a long time ago."

"Katy..."

She ignored him, frowning intently in the darkness as she worked through her shaky logic. Slowly the spinning chaos that had invaded her mind on the night of her wedding settled, allowing her to view her situation more rationally for the first time. "You're right about a lot of things, Garrett. We could be a good team. We have common interests and mutual respect and, until our wedding night, we had what I thought was a good friendship."

"Katy, honey, we do have all those things—that's what I've been trying to tell you for the past few days." Garrett's voice sounded unnaturally husky in the darkness. His big hands flexed on the wheel and then regripped it more tightly than before. "I'm sorry your wedding night didn't live up to your expectations. It was my fault. I was tired, and by the time we got into bed I was aching for you. It had been a long time since I had, well, been with a woman." He brushed that subject aside. "At any rate, I moved too fast. I know that now. I should have taken more time to make it good for you. And then I fell asleep on you. That was stupid. It was just that I got the impression you didn't want any more, uh, lovemaking, that night and I . . . Never mind. Let's just say I know I didn't handle things well and I'm sorry. If you'll give me another chance I'll do my best to make it good for you—I swear it."

Katy stared at his shadowed profile. Her own embarrassment was overcome by a realization of what he had been thinking for several days. "Garrett, what on earth are you talking about? It *was* good for me. I told you that. In fact, it was unbelievable. I had no idea I could feel such sensations. You're a...a fantastic lover." Flushing furiously now, Katy stared fixedly out the window.

Garrett took his eyes off the road long enough to pin her with a glittering glance. "If I were all that fantastic, we would never have gotten into this mess. You wouldn't have had so many doubts and uncertainties. You wouldn't have awakened hating me."

"Garrett, I don't hate you." Katy stared at him, shocked that he could have come to such a conclusion.

"Do you have any idea what I've been going through since our wedding night?"

"I know, Garrett." She stared into the rain.

"For God's sake, honey, I—"

Whatever he was going to say next was lost forever as Garrett hit the brakes with lightning-swift reflexes.

Katy saw the huge, dark shape lunge from the gully out into the middle of the road in the same instant that Garrett saw it and reacted. For a few blinding seconds the headlights illuminated a very wide-awake-looking Red Dazzle.

The horse stood, trembling and tense in the center of the narrow road as the Mercedes slammed to a halt less than a couple of feet away. Lightning flashed. The frightened animal shuddered, gathered himself and dashed toward the opposite side of the pavement. An instant later he bounded up the short incline and vanished in the blinding rain.

"It's Red," Katy whispered, horrified. "We almost hit him."

"If we'd been going any faster, we would have hit him."

"All three of us would have wound up in the emergency room," Katy murmured.

"Or the morgue. Thirteen hundred pounds of horseflesh and a Mercedes don't mix well." Garrett's voice was savage as he pulled the car to the side of the road and switched off the engine. "How the hell did he get out? I checked the stall door myself before we left tonight."

"We'll have to go after him. He's scared and he's lost. He could wander out in front of another car."

"I'll go after him," Garrett said. He reached into the back seat and picked up a length of rope. "You drive the car back to the house."

"I'll help you find him first." Katy shoved the handle on the car door. "In his present condition it might take two of us to round him up and get a rope attached."

"Stop it, Katy, you'll ruin your clothes. I can handle this."

But Katy was already out of the car, and she was rapidly getting drenched. "Too late. My clothes are already ruined. Lucky I wear flat shoes, isn't it? Imagine having to tromp around in this mud in a pair of heels."

"Katy, so help me . . ."

But Katy was already starting across the road, following the direction Red Dazzle had taken. With a muttered oath, Garrett grabbed a flashlight and went after her.

Katy heard him give a low, piercing whistle in the darkness as they scrambled up the small incline.

"Does this trick pony of yours come when you call?" she asked as they plowed through a cluster of wet bushes.

"If he feels like it."

"Maybe his normal dormant state will overtake him before he gets very far. I must admit, he didn't look particularly sleepy a minute ago, though."

"No," Garrett said thoughtfully, "he looked downright spooked. It takes a heck of a lot to spook old Red."

"The lightning storm might have done it."

"Yeah. The question is, what was he doing out in the first place?"

"Vandals? Pranksters?" Katy suggested. "Or a broken lock on the stall door?"

"Damned if I know," Garrett muttered as he swung the arc of the light through the rainy darkness. "But I sure intend to find out." He gave the low whistle again.

"I don't hear the thundering hooves of a big red horse returning to his master's call," Katy noted.

"He's not Trigger."

A moving shadow caught Katy's eye. A low, questioning wicker came through the darkness.

"Over there, Garrett."

"I saw him. You go left and circle slowly in from the other side. Don't make any sudden moves. Just ease in on him."

"I know how to handle a spooked horse."

Garrett grinned briefly. "Sorry. Guess I forgot who I had married. Go get 'em, cowgirl."

Katy wrinkled her nose but said nothing as she moved off into the rain.

The process didn't take long. Red Dazzle seemed relieved more than anything else once he realized who had come after him. His ears came to attention as he identified his old rodeo pal, and after a few muffled snorts and assorted irritated comments he ambled toward Garrett and allowed the rope to be attached to the halter.

Katy's flanking movement proved unnecessary. By the time she emerged beside Garrett and the horse, it was clear Red Dazzle was disgusted with his night out in the rain and longed only to get home.

"I know the feeling," Garrett said as Red Dazzle prodded his shoulder. "It's time we all went home."

He abruptly reached out and clamped a hand around the nape of Katy's neck. Her wet hair spilled over his fingers. Pulling her toward him, he kissed her soundly on the mouth and then vaulted lightly up on his horse's back. "I'll ride him back. You bring the car. As soon as you get home, hop into a hot shower."

"All right."

Garrett saw her safely behind the wheel. As she started to close the door he leaned down. "Drive carefully, Katy. We're not far from the house but this road is dangerous on a night like this."

"Yes, Garrett." It was sweet of him to be protective, Katy decided. From now on she would take comfort from such things.

"I'll see you in a few minutes."

Katy gave one last obedient nod and closed the car door. She sat silently for a moment, savoring the taste of Garrett's kiss as she watched Red Dazzle move off down the road. The horse was responding to the invisible pressure signals Garrett gave with his knees. Old Red might appear to be half asleep most of the time, but he was, in fact, beautifully trained. Garrett didn't even need a bridle to guide him.

Man and horse vanished into the rain, taking a shortcut back to the barn, and Katy reached out to switch on the ignition. She drove slowly back to the big house, her mind filled with the import of the decision she had made.

In a way it was like deciding to get married all over again, she thought. Then she smiled wryly. Not quite. This time around, it had been harder to make the decision. She knew she was allowing her love for Garrett to guide her, and the logical part of her brain warned that such guidance might be suspect.

She was stepping willingly back into an intimate relationship with a man who did not love her. This time around, she knew the facts, yet she was making the same decision.

She was going to take the risk because a part of her refused to give up on Garrett Coltrane.

He might not know how to love, but there was great depth to the man. It was, Katy decided with jubilant anticipation, entirely possible that he could learn how to love.

And who better to teach him than a wife, she asked herself as she parked in the driveway. Irrational optimism surged through her as she bounded out of the car and dashed for the front steps.

There was a light on down at the stable, she noted. Garrett and Red Dazzle had arrived. It would be a while before Garrett got back to the house. The horse had to be dried off and settled for the night. Katy decided to follow orders.

It seemed very bold and adventurous to walk into the master bedroom and strip off her wet clothes. During the past few days she had come to think of this room as Garrett's. She glanced around as she walked nude into the adjoining bath. In the few days he had been occupying the bedroom, Garrett had somehow managed to put his stamp on it. She could see the two contrasting sides of the man as she studied the room.

The closet contained both faded jeans and expensively cut business suits. Scuffed boots were lined up next to fine dress shoes that had been polished to a high gloss. Hanging from a hook were several belts of thin, supple leather designed to go with the suits. Dangling alongside was a wide, gaudily tooled strip of leather that ended in a huge flashy silver buckle. The big buckle was engraved with words that immortalized Garrett's championship status as a rodeo cowboy.

Garrett Coltrane had come a long way since the days he had cleaned out her father's stables, Katy acknowledged. He'd learned a lot but he'd never learned how to love. A lot of factors had been working against him, she told herself charitably. For one thing he'd had poor teachers in his parents and a bad experience with a woman who used an artificial form of love to satisfy her craving for excitement. In addition to those factors, vaulting up several rungs on the ladder of success and respectability was bound to have taken a tremendous amount of drive and energy. There would have been very little left over for the softer things in life. But maybe it was not too late for Garrett to learn about love.

Katy walked on into the bath, turned on the shower and stepped under the hot spray.

She was just beginning to relax under the warm water when a change in the atmosphere warned her that someone had opened the bathroom door. Her fingers tightened nervously around the bar of soap she was holding.

"Garrett?"

The shower door opened abruptly, and Katy gave a small squeak. Garrett stood there, his eyes drinking in the sight of her as she stood beneath the cascading water. He had undressed, and he seemed to fill the shower entrance. He was already fully, magnificently aroused. When he stepped inside and closed the door behind him, muscle rippled smoothly under the hard planes of his shoulders and flanks.

"This is supposed to be romantic," Garrett said, still staring at her.

"What is?" Instinctively she held the washcloth over her breasts and then realized how little she was hiding. She smiled tremulously.

"Taking a shower together." His mouth curved slightly as he put his hands behind her neck and tipped up her chin with his thumbs. "I think I could get used to some of this romantic stuff."

"I have great faith in your adaptability." Katy's eyes were luminous. She splayed her fingers on his wet chest, enjoying the rough texture of the hair that covered him there. She could feel and see him responding to her, and the knowledge that she had such an effect on him made her light-headed. Her shyness melted quickly, just as it had the first time Garrett had taken her in his arms.

Garrett let his hands slide down to cup her shoulders. His eyes were brilliant and intense as he looked at her. "Katy, honey, you won't regret giving us another chance, I swear it. We belong together. We're right for each other. We've got everything going for us, and we're going to make it work."

"You seem very sure of that."

"I wouldn't have married you if I wasn't sure. I know what I want, and I'm willing to work to get it. You're a hard worker, too. I know you are. All I'm asking is that you put in some effort to make our marriage work."

She cradled his face between her soft palms. "It seems little enough to ask, doesn't it?" She urged his head down to hers and parted her lips invitingly.

"Katy, my sweet Katy." His voice was a muffled groan of desire as his mouth closed hungrily over hers.

Katy felt the trembling in Garrett's muscles as he sought to hold himself in check. She was touched by his obvious effort not to rush matters.

"This time I want a chance to explore you," she whispered against his wet chest.

"Yes, Katy, honey, anything you want. Anything. Take your time. I want you to touch every part of me." His hands slipped heavily down her back to her hips.

He cupped her in his palms, squeezing gently. "I want you to know me. I want you to be comfortable with me. I want you to learn me so well you'll never want to go to a stranger." The words came in a deep, aching, husky tone.

Now that he was holding her again, Katy admitted to herself that she couldn't imagine going to any other man. "You're the only one I want to touch. There's no one else I could possibly want. No one." Her fingertips moved over his water-slick shoulders.

"Ah, Katy, that feels so good." He shuddered heavily and urged her closer. His fingers tightened under her rounded buttocks, and he lifted her up against him. "Look what you do to me."

"I can feel what I'm doing to you." She clung to him, her arms around his neck and gloried in the strength of his body. He was hard and strong and tight with his need.

His fingers flexed strongly. Katy cried out softly as a wave of excitement swept through her. She buried her face in the curve of his shoulder, tasting him with the tip of her tongue as the water poured over both of them.

"Slow down, honey. I want to do this right." Garrett groaned as Katy wriggled against him. His body throbbed against hers in response.

"Stop worrying about doing it right. You're doing just fine." She laughed softly.

"What's so funny?" he demanded.

"Nothing," she said quickly and then smiled as she dipped her head to nip his shoulder. Her small white teeth tantalized him.

"*Katy.*"

"I was just thinking that it seems strange for me to be reassuring you. You always seem to know what you're doing and how you're going to do it."

"Not with you, apparently. I think I've made some mistakes with you, sweetheart."

She laughed up at him with her eyes. "Not in this department, you didn't."

His smile was slow and infinitely sexy as he eased her down the length of him until she was standing on her feet again. Then he reached around her to turn off the shower.

"If this is the one thing I'm good at," he murmured as he led her out of the shower and reached for a towel, "then I'd better concentrate on doing it well."

Katy closed her eyes, enjoying a deep, sensual pleasure that was still new to her as Garrett caressed her slowly and thoroughly with the towel. He used the rough side of the terry cloth to tease her nipples, and when he was satisfied with their tight, budlike appearance, he leaned down and kissed each with great care.

"Do you like that, Katy?"

"Yes," she said, her voice husky with desire. "Yes, I like it very much."

"Tell me what else you like. Please, Katy. Tell me what you want me to do."

"Everything you do feels right." She slid her hand down to his flat stomach and then went lower, cupping him intimately.

Garrett's breath hissed between his teeth. "Oh, God, Katy."

"I'm doing all right?"

"You're doing perfectly. Too perfectly. I'm about to explode."

"So am I."

Garrett finished drying both of them, taking as much time as he could with the process. He lingered over every curve and valley. When he was finished Katy could hardly stand. She wrapped her arms around him.

"Hold me," she pleaded.

"I'll hold you, Katy." He picked her up and carried her into the other room, setting her down on the bed he had turned back on his way into the bathroom. "I'll hold you so tight and so close that you'll never want to leave."

He came down beside her, parting her legs with his own so he could sink his fingers into her silken, liquid warmth. Katy twisted at the intimate touch, reaching out to pull him closer.

Garrett resisted, using his hands and lips to coax the response he wanted from her. He was so intent on pleasuring her, Katy thought bemusedly. It seemed to be the only thing he cared about in the whole world. Once again he was focused completely on her, and the sensation was dazzling.

In the end both of them were shivering in each other's arms, feverish with the passionate need that drove them. Katy surrendered willingly once more to the strong, primitive storm that swept into existence just long enough to catch man and woman and bind them together for a split-second glimpse of eternity.

# 7

THE NEXT MORNING Red Dazzle looked none the worse for his adventure during the night. Garrett lounged against the bottom half of the stall door and watched the stocky horse contentedly munch hay. The red tail swished idly, and the surprisingly sensitive ears rotated with mild curiosity as Garrett spoke a few soft words. The powerful jaws never ceased their steady chewing action as Red Dazzle worked his way through breakfast. Red had set his priorities early in life. Food was at the top of the list, closely followed by napping.

"I reckon we both had ourselves one heck of an exciting night last night, didn't we, Red?" Garrett's mouth curved into a wickedly complacent grin as he recalled his own private adventures in bed. "On the whole, though, I'll bet I had a better time than you did."

Red Dazzle favored Garrett with a brief, sidelong glance but didn't stop eating.

Garrett was feeling extraordinarily good that morning. He hadn't felt so good in a long time. "I've got me one sweet, sexy little wife, Red. You'd never know it to look at her. On the surface she's calm and polite and serious and just a little shy. But in bed she turns into a waterfall made out of fire. Soft as a kitten, wild as a filly who's never had a saddle on her. You never saw anything like it."

Red twitched his tail again and used his mobile lips to tug free a particularly tasty clump of hay. He was obviously not impressed with human sexuality.

Garrett shrugged, not offended by Red's lack of interest in the wonders of married life. "There are times when I feel sorry for you, Red. Being a gelding has its drawbacks."

Garrett went back to work, whistling softly between his teeth as he examined the stall door closure. The metal mechanism appeared to be in perfect condition. There was no obvious explanation for how the door had accidentally opened last night.

The sun was shining crisp and clear. All traces of the storm had vanished, leaving behind a fresh, glistening fall morning. The day felt new and full of promise.

Just like his marriage.

Garrett experienced a sense of deep satisfaction at the thought. The brief, astonishing, totally unexpected storm that had erupted the morning after the wedding appeared to be over as quickly as it had begun. Katy was back to normal. Everything was going to be all right. It was going to work out just the way he had originally planned. Better than he had planned, Garrett decided cheerfully. When he had first decided to marry Katy, he hadn't realized just how much of a woman he would be getting. He hadn't known how lucky he was going to be.

"You're fortunate you don't have to worry about the female psyche, Red. I'm telling you, it's a maze. Even the intelligent, sensible-looking ones can surprise you. Who would have thought sweet, gentle little Katy would have gone all stubborn and temperamental the way she did the day after we got married? Bridal jitters, they call it, but I'll tell you, for the past few days I felt like I was the one walking through a mine field. But it's all over now. Things are back to normal."

Red sighed gustily in agreement and reached for more hay.

"I'm going to have to keep an eye on her, though," Garrett confided to the gelding. "I saw the way Hutton and a few of the others looked at her last night. Every time she opened her mouth about breeding programs, she had a male audience hanging on every word. I don't think she realized just how sexy she is when she starts talking about confirmation, pedigrees and fertility. She gets so serious and intent and the nearest males start thinking of themselves as studs. When she launched into a discussion of the advantages of natural breeding over artificial insemination, I thought I was going to have to hog tie her and carry her out of the room. Every man listening to her was salivating. The funny part is, I don't think she even realized it."

Red Dazzle, who saved his salivating for his feed, twitched his ears and went on chewing energetically. Garrett went back to whistling while he played with the stall door lock. It was Emmett Bracken's sour, hung-over greeting that made him glance up a few minutes later. The man had obviously tied one on the night before.

"Morning, Mr. Coltrane." Emmett came into the small stable carrying a pitchfork. "How's it going?"

Garrett nodded, a brief, casual greeting. "There was a problem with this stall door last night."

Emmett frowned, his leathery features seaming into countless small lines. His faded eyes narrowed. "What kind of problem?"

"Old Red here got out. I nearly hit him on the road coming back from Hutton's party."

"He was on the road?"

"Yeah. Spooked by the storm. Or something. I almost didn't see him in time."

Emmett pursed his lips and gazed thoughtfully at Red Dazzle. "Is the hardware on the door okay?"

"The door's fine."

"He's one smart old horse. Been around. Any chance he figured out how to open that latch himself?" Emmett asked slowly.

"No," Garrett said bluntly. "There's no chance he got it open himself. He's smart but he doesn't have hands. It took a pair of hands to get this door open."

"Or a pair of hands to forget to close it properly last night," Emmett pointed out in a neutral-sounding voice.

"I checked it myself around six o'clock."

There was a long silence. Emmett stood holding the pitchfork, staring at the latch on the stall door. "You figure someone opened it deliberately?"

"The thought had crossed my mind." Garrett watched Emmett closely.

The old man shook his head and straightened his worn cap so the brim of the hat came down low over his eyes and shielded his gaze. "I guess it could have happened that way."

"What way?" Garrett prodded.

Emmett shrugged. "Could have been deliberate."

"You know something I don't know, Bracken?" Garrett asked very softly.

"I know that horse means a lot to you. Anyone who's been around you very long knows that much," Emmett said cryptically.

Garrett folded his arms and leaned back against the stall door. "What are you trying to say, Bracken?"

"Just that someone with a grudge against you might have decided to go after old Red." Emmett started to turn away.

"Bracken." Garrett didn't move, but Emmett stopped as if he'd been jerked to a halt.

"I don't know anything you don't know, Coltrane." Emmett rubbed the back of his neck in a nervous fashion.

"Meaning?"

"Meaning that you know the people who got grudges against you better than I do."

"Maybe," Garrett said dryly, "But I'd like to hear you name a few, just the same."

Emmett gave a grim snort, and his hand clenched around the handle of the pitchfork. "If I were you, I'd start with the females on the list. A woman who feels she'd been wronged will do some mighty strange things. Or haven't you lived long enough to know that fact of life yet?" Emmett walked out of the stable.

Katy heard Emmett's voice as she was just about to step into the stable. She moved aside as he strode past her.

"'Scuse me, ma'am. Didn't see you." Bracken kept moving, not pausing to greet her.

Katy smiled fleetingly at the man's back. She was growing accustomed to Emmett Bracken's morose ways. Then she went toward Garrett who was regarding her with a curious expression. "Hi. I came to see how Red Dazzle looks this morning."

"He's fine." Garrett continued to study her thoughtfully.

Katy swallowed, suddenly uncomfortable under that steady gaze. Her heart plunged. She had spent most of the night convincing herself that she was doing the right thing by agreeing to make the marriage a real one. Now, with a single unreadable glance from her husband, she was forced to wonder if she'd made another mistake. Garrett looked grim and aloof this morning. Not at all the way he had looked during the night.

"Is something wrong, Garrett?"

"Emmett and I were just discussing the fact that the only way Red could have gotten free last night was with a little human help."

"What?" Katy was startled. "Someone let him out?"

"Looks that way."

"But who?"

"That," Garrett said quietly, "is the interesting part of the question."

"Kids playing dangerous pranks? Or some vagrant who wanted to spend the night in a warm stable?"

"Emmett suggested a woman might have done it," Garrett said. "He implied that trying to hurt Red was the kind of revenge a woman might take against a man she felt had wronged her."

Katy caught her breath and reached out to brace herself against the wall of the stable. The full import of what he had just said struck her with the impact of a slap. Instinctively she recoiled.

"You think I had something to do with this?" Katy whispered. "You think I would do such a thing? After . . . after what happened between us last night?"

Garrett studied her a moment longer. "Red was set free several hours before you and I went to bed. There's no telling exactly when he did get out."

"Garrett!"

"He could have been killed. He could have blundered over the cliffs during that storm. Or he could have been hit by a truck. Hell, I almost killed him myself. That would have been a rather vicious piece of revenge, wouldn't it?"

"Garrett, for heaven's sake." Katy's nails were biting into the palm of her hand. She couldn't believe this was happening. "Do you really think I would do such a thing just because I didn't like the way my marriage turned out? Do you think I would take my revenge out on a horse?"

Garrett straightened and took a step toward her. His big hands closed around her shoulders as he looked down at her with an intensity that made Katy shiver. It was obvious he had come to some inner decision.

"No," he said roughly, "I don't believe you would use old Red to take revenge against me. Bracken's wrong. A woman who feels she'd got a right to a grudge might do some strange things, but one thing's for certain: I know a few things about you, and one of those things is that you love horses. You would never put one at risk the way Red was put at risk last night. You wouldn't use a horse to get even with me. You're an honest woman, Katy. You fight your own battles."

Katy went limp under his hands. "Well, thank you for that much, at least."

Garrett groaned and pulled her against him. He wrapped his arms around her and spoke into her hair. "I'm sorry, Katy. For a few minutes there, after Emmett implied it could have been a woman, all I could think of was how upset you've been since the wedding. For days I didn't know what you were thinking or feeling. You seemed different from the Katy I thought I knew. All that foolishness about living together as if we were roommates or business partners or something was enough to make a man feel as if he'd just stepped down the rabbit hole in *Alice in Wonderland*. I didn't know what was going on."

Some of Katy's immediate sense of relief began to fade. "Obviously it doesn't take much to completely baffle the male brain."

"We're simple, straightforward creatures, Katy. Just ask any man." He was smiling.

Katy put her arms around his waist and leaned her head against his broad chest. The tension seeped slowly out of her. "All right. If we're agreed that it wasn't me who let Red out last night, who is the culprit?"

Garrett shook his head. "Damned if I know. Probably a prankster, like you said. Or some kid who just wanted to pet the nice horsey or take a joy ride. In any event, I'm going to see it doesn't happen again."

Katy lifted her head to look up at him. "How?"

"I'm going to put an alarm system on the stable this afternoon. Nothing complicated. Just something that will set off some bells in the house if someone decides to open the stable door after it's been closed for the night. That should be enough to take care of any kids or troublemakers who come nosing around."

Katy nodded. "I'm sorry you thought it might have been me, even for a moment, Garrett."

He hugged her fiercely and then stepped back. He left one arm draped possessively around her shoulders. "You've had me so confused for the past few days I haven't known which end was up, lady. But everything's back to normal now." He looked down at her, eyes gleaming with memories of the night. "Isn't it?"

Katy smiled tremulously, her own memories making her blush warmly. "I'm not sure what normal is supposed to feel like, Garrett."

"As long as it feels like last night, we'll do fine." Amusement and satisfaction were heavy in his voice. He was a man who was back in complete charge of his own private universe. "You know, I've been thinking, Katy."

"I understand that's a dangerous thing for a man to attempt."

He gave her an affectionate shake. "Don't get sassy. I'm serious. You and I have a lot in common, and we should take advantage of that fact. It's good for a marriage."

"Since when did you become such an expert on marriage?" Katy leaned into the stall to survey Red Dazzle, who took a few seconds out from his busy schedule to blow into her palm. Katy smiled and glanced up at Garrett out of the corner of her eye. To her surprise he was taking the question seriously.

"I'll admit I'm learning as I go along. But it makes good sense to share things, Katy. One of the reasons we got married was because we have a lot of mutual interests."

"I suppose it was." She concentrated on Red Dazzle, wondering what was coming next. She might have succeeded in baffling Garrett on a few occasions lately, but that was nothing compared to what he was capable of doing to her.

"We should take advantage of those mutual interests."

"Okay, I'll buy that," Katy said agreeably.

"I think it's time somebody threw you back up on a horse, Katy."

Katy went rigid. She clung to the stall door, staring blindly at the red horse inside. "Forget it."

"Now, Katy, honey, it's time you were reasonable about this." Garrett's voice took on a rich, soothing quality. He gentled Katy with his hand, stroking her the way he would a nervous mare. "I know all about what happened to you during that barn fire. I know about how long you spent getting well. But that's all in the past. I talked to your father at the wedding about it and we agreed. Riding used to be a big part of your life. It's wrong to just abandon it because you had a bad experience."

"A bad experience! Garrett, I nearly died." Katy swung around. "You can't even imagine what it was like that night. The smoke and the flames and the terrified animals. And the pain. Garrett, do you have any idea how much I hurt afterward? Can't you understand?"

"Honey, I understand. But if you'd had a car accident, you would have had to learn to get back into a car sooner or later. This is no different."

"This is different. I have a choice and I've chosen not to ride ever again. Don't lecture me, Garrett. I made my decision a long time ago. I'm an adult and I have a right to make my own decisions."

"You've let yourself develop a phobia about it. But riding was something special to you," Garrett persisted. "I remember how you looked when you were in a saddle. You came alive on a horse, the same way you do when you're in my arms."

Katy flushed. "For heaven's sake, Garrett, that's a ridiculous analogy. How would you remember how I looked? I was just a kid when you knew me all those years ago."

He smiled whimsically, his fingers toying with a tendril of her hair. "I remember, Katy. I remember how much you liked the blue ribbons and the excitement of the show ring. I remember how intense and serious you were during a show and how elated you were afterward. I remember all the hours you spent getting a horse ready for the ring. And I remember how gutsy you were. Riding was the most important thing in your life in those days. You were very, very good."

"People change, Garrett. You should know that as well as anyone."

"I agree. People change. But some things don't change. You love horses and you were a beautiful rider once upon a time. Riding is something you and I can do together. It's something we have in common. It's time you got back on a horse. You've spent too many years building up the fear in your mind until it's way out of proportion." Garrett smiled warmly. "I'm going to help you get over that old fear."

"Don't push me, Garrett."

"You'll thank me for it later, honey."

Katy's eyes widened in anger and exasperation. "Don't you dare patronize me. Garrett, so help me, if you don't—"

"Hush," he said, leaning down to kiss her lightly on the mouth. "Take it easy, honey. I'm not going to rush you into anything. We'll take our time, I promise. Just like we took our time last night." Deliberately he deepened the kiss. "You taste good," he muttered against her parted lips.

"You're trying to distract me," Katy accused, her fear and exasperation dissolving beneath the warmth of his kiss. Her mouth opened instinctively for his sensual invasion. The night before she had decided that if this was the one area in which they could truly communicate, then her only option lay in trying to facilitate that communication. The problem with that decision was that she faced many moments such as this, moments in which she was afraid she surrendered too much of herself into the hands of a man who had not yet learned to love her. The risk she ran was enormous and she knew it.

"I like distracting you." He eased her back against the stable wall, planting his hands on either side of her and caging her with his body. He moved his knee between her legs, and when she gave way to the insistent pressure he thrust his thigh intimately between hers. "That's it, honey. Tighten your legs around me the same way you would around a stallion. Ride me."

Katy was torn between a surge of desire and a surge of panic. "Garrett! Someone will see us. Emmett is nearby. He could come back at any time."

"Not if he knows what's good for him," Garrett muttered. "But since you're still such a shy little thing, I guess I better ensure some privacy."

"What are you going to do?"

"Guess." He scooped her up and tossed her lightly over his shoulder.

"We can't! Not here. Put me down, Garrett. Do you hear me?"

"I hear you." Garrett was carrying her into the empty stall where straw and hay were stored. He closed the stall door firmly behind them. They were instantly in shadow. Golden sunlight seeped through the cracks in the wooden walls. Garrett lowered Katy slowly into the straw. "Your problem is that you still haven't gotten accustomed to being a wife yet."

"Is that right?" She looked up at him from beneath her lashes as he loomed over her. She could feel the gathering sexual tension in him, and it thrilled her to know she had this effect on him. "I suppose you figure it's your job to help me get accustomed to my role?"

"My solemn duty and responsibility," he assured her as he came down on top of her. His eyes were brilliant in the gloom of the shadowed stall, as brilliant as they had been during the long night.

Katy sighed softly and put her arms around him, drawing him down to her. When he looked at her like that, she let her hopes and dreams sweep through her and take command of her senses.

Garrett dealt impatiently with their clothing, flinging jeans and shirts into a careless pile. Then he moved onto his back, nestling against the discarded clothing and grasped Katy by the waist. His aroused body was taut with desire, and she was suddenly, violently ready for him. He touched her lingeringly, testing the moist warmth between her legs, and when she moaned, he growled his pleasure.

Slowly, he eased Katy down on top of him, sheathing himself within her. Katy gasped and trembled in his hands.

"Show me how good a rider you are," he said in a dark, husky voice.

Then he laughed with soft triumph as her fingers bit into the hard, muscled skin of his shoulders. A few minutes later he was no longer laughing.

The passion captured them both.


A LONG TIME LATER Katy felt Garrett stir beneath her. With a sigh, she reluctantly eased herself off him. He swore with great depth of feeling and winced as he sat up beside her.

"Remind me to think twice before I try this again." Garrett brushed straw off himself and handed Katy her clothes. "A man could do himself permanent injury making love on straw."

Katy pulled a piece of straw out of her hair and smiled wistfully. "I thought it was kind of romantic."

Garrett stepped into his jeans and fastened them quickly. "That's because you were on top."

"Don't blame me. It was your idea." Katy concentrated on doing up her shirt.

"Hey." Garrett reached down and tipped up her chin. "I was just teasing you." He searched her face, his expression intently curious. "Did you really think it was romantic?"

Katy hesitated and then nodded once, briefly.

Garrett grinned suddenly, obviously pleased with himself. "Well, how about that? I never would have thought . . . Never mind. You thought it was romantic, huh?"

"Umm-hmm." Katy wondered at his look of pride.

"In that case, maybe we will try it again sometime. A man has to be prepared to make certain sacrifices for his woman."

Katy smiled in spite of herself. "Is that right?"

"Damned right." Garrett finished buttoning his shirt and watched with lazy, possessive interest as Katy pulled on her clothing more slowly. Then his grin faded and his expression grew more serious again.

"Is something wrong?" Katy eyed him warily.

"I was just thinking about Bracken's suggestion that a woman might have let Red out last night."

Katy's head came up abruptly. Pain and fear knifed through her. "Are we back to that again? What is this? Now that you've had your morning fling in the straw, you've decided to start wondering if I might be the guilty party, after all?"

Garrett's eyes narrowed warningly. "Calm down. You sure are jumpy lately. Downright temperamental. I wasn't thinking it might have been you who opened the door. I know damned well it wasn't. It was something else that was bothering me."

"What?"

"I was just wondering where Bracken got the idea that it might have been you who did it. He said something about a woman feeling wronged."

Katy stared at him for a moment. Then her eyes slid away. "I can guess where he got the idea."

"Yeah? Suppose you share your guesses with me."
There was a soft challenge in Garret's words.

Katy sighed. "Nadine has noticed our . . . our sleeping arrangements. She's been working in the house with me, getting things organized. She knows we've been using separate bedrooms. That's a bit odd for two people who are on their honeymoon. She also overheard our argument yesterday after Royce Hutton left. I suspect she drew her own conclusions about the state of our marriage and passed them along to her husband."

"I see." Garrett opened the stall door. "It makes sense. You have been acting like a woman wronged lately, haven't you?"

Katy glared at him. "I hadn't noticed."

Garrett's mouth curved humorously, and he reached out to ruffle her hair. "So that's where Bracken got his ideas this morning. But that's all over, isn't it, Katy? We've got this marriage back on course, and it's going to stay there. No more emotional storms or tantrums. No more cases of extended bridal jitters."

Katy raised her eyebrows and pitched her voice into tones of artificially sweet docility. "Whatever you say, Garrett." It gave her an odd feeling to tease him.

Garrett laughed, hugged her fiercely and kissed the top of her head. "Come on, lady, let's go get a cup of coffee and something to eat. Any of those muffins left over from breakfast?"

"You just ate an hour ago."

"I seem to have worked up an appetite."

But the phone was ringing when they walked into the kitchen. Garrett gave an impatient exclamation and reached for it. Katy listened to the one-sided conversation and knew that something serious had happened at the Fresno office at Coltrane and Company, something that had Garrett's instant attention. As he spoke into the receiver, he watched Katy bustle around the kitchen.

"All right, Carson, calm down. Is Layton there? What the hell do you mean, he's on vacation? Get hold of him and tell him to get back to the office." There was a pause and then Garrett swore softly. "Okay, okay, I hear you. He can't be reached. Damn. Next time the man takes a week off, make sure he goes someplace where they have telephones. Sounds like I'll have to come on over." He glanced at his watch. "I can be there by late afternoon. Tell Bisby to sit tight. The bank can't move as fast as we can. He's not going to lose his land in the next forty-eight hours. He'll get his loan. See you by three o'clock. Now pay attention, Carson. Here's what I want you to do while you're waiting for me."

Katy listened to Garrett rattle off a terse list of instructions that displayed a fine knowledge of how bankers and accountants worked and thought. Then he hung up the phone with a loud, irritated clatter. He reached for the cup of coffee Katy had set in front of him.

"You heard?" he asked.

"You're going to drive to Fresno this afternoon?" Katy sat down across from him and wrapped her hands around her own mug. She delicately blew on the hot brew.

"Afraid so. They're short staffed this month, and the head of the office, Layton, is on vacation somewhere in the wilds of Mexico. Can't be reached. One of our clients is in trouble with the IRS and the bank. Everyone's running around screaming foreclosure. Normally I wouldn't have to get involved in something like this unless it got a lot worse, but in this case it looks like I'd better go on over and get things calmed down."

Katy nodded. "It will be a good opportunity for me to see the inner workings of one of your offices. Will we be staying overnight?"

Garrett blinked at her over the rim of the coffee cup. Then he shook his head firmly. "I'll be staying overnight. You'll be staying here. There's no reason for you to come with me. I'll be back tomorrow. We're still on our honeymoon, remember?"

Katy smiled tentatively. "Yes, I know, but this marriage is supposed to be a working partnership. You made that very clear right from the beginning. This is a perfect opportunity for me to start learning my new job."

He shot her a glowering look. "There'll be plenty of opportunity for you to learn the ins and outs of Coltrane and Company after we've had our honeymoon."

"Why postpone the learning session, Garrett? It makes sense for me to go with you today. I'll get a chance to meet the people in the Fresno office, and I'll see how things function in a crisis."

"A crisis is no time to learn a new job." Garrett's tone had a hard edge. He picked up a muffin and took a savage bite out of it. "You'd just be in the way."

Katy bit her lip, a little hurt and a little angry. "I'll stay out of your way."

"You'll stay here," he exploded. "Dammit, you're supposed to be a new bride. You're not supposed to have to start worrying about a new job at this stage."

"Why not?" Katy shot back, her temper fracturing. "It's the reason you hired me, isn't it? To go to work for Coltrane and Company?"

*"Hired you."* Garrett's coffee cup came down with a crash. He stared at her. "Hired you? What the hell are you talking about? I didn't hire you, I married you, woman!"

Katy winced. "Sorry, it was just a slip of the tongue."

"A slip of the tongue?" Garrett was incredulous. "You get the word 'hire' mixed up with the word 'marry' and you call it a slip of the tongue?"

"Calm down, Garrett. I told you, it was a simple mistake." One she was rapidly regretting, Katy thought dismally.

"Like hell." He got to his feet, his face thunderous. "Let's get one thing clear, Katy Coltrane—that wasn't an employment application you filled out a couple of weeks ago, it was a marriage license application. This isn't a probationary training period you're in at the moment, it's a honeymoon. You're my wife, not my employee. Try to figure out just what that means during the next twenty-four hours, will you?"

"Garrett . . ."

"I'm going to get hold of a guy I know who does home security work. I want something installed on that stable this afternoon."

He stalked out of the kitchen, leaving Katy feeling as though she had just tangled with a tornado. Her fingers were trembling as she lifted her cup of coffee again.

Slowly she took a long, soothing sip. When she set down her cup again, she was smiling very slightly to herself. If she had looked in a mirror, her eyes would have sparkled back at her.

Teaching Garrett Coltrane how to love was a risky business, but she thought she had prepared herself for most of the hazards involved.

What she hadn't prepared herself for was the discovery of her own spirited, unexpectedly bold nature. There was something exhilarating about challenging Garrett, even when she lost. Just as there was something very exhilarating about making love to him.

One way or another, the man was finally beginning to notice her.

She hadn't felt like this since the last time she had ridden one of her father's Arabians to a blue ribbon.

# 8

THE BIG HOUSE felt empty and lonely that night. Katy poured herself a glass of wine and cooked a light dinner, which she ate in the kitchen. She turned the television on for the evening news but turned it off again later when it became annoying. She read for a while and finally treated herself to a nightcap of brandy. It was going to be a long night.

The master bedroom at the end of the hall seemed very large and forbiddingly formal when she finally wandered into it around ten o'clock. The room needed Garrett's earthy, masculine presence to counteract its designer perfection, Katy decided as she undressed slowly and crawled into bed. Garrett had a way of making a room his when he was in it.

He also had a way of dominating a bed when he was in it. Katy felt very much alone as she curled up on her side of the huge bed. It was strange, she thought. She had only spent one night in this bed with her husband, but apparently she had gotten addicted to his presence in it already. It seemed very empty without him sprawled beside her like a lazily sensual lion. She wondered if Garrett would take some satisfaction from knowing that she missed him. She hoped he was missing her tonight.

It didn't take any great amount of intuition to figure out the real reason he hadn't wanted to take her with him to Fresno. Katy sensed that in his own, very male, very chauvinistic and rather convoluted fashion, he was trying to turn her into a wife before he turned her into a business associate. It was touching, in a way. He was nervous about allowing her to get involved in her new job while certain matters were still unresolved in their relationship.

She wasn't sure if Garrett himself realized exactly how his logic was working, but Katy took heart from the muddle-headed approach he was using. She smiled to herself. On some level he recognized that their relationship was more important than their business association, and he wanted it firmly established.

One of these days Garrett might even realize he was in love.

As if on cue, the phone on the nightstand burbled plaintively. Katy picked it up.

"Hello?"

"Hi, Katy." Garrett sounded alert. It was obvious he wasn't just about to crawl into bed. "Thought I'd check in and see how things were going with you."

Katy sat up against the pillows and switched on the light. "I'm fine. I just got into bed. How are things there?"

"Fresno is Fresno. But the client's going to survive. Barely. I saw the bankers personally this afternoon and got a reprieve. Tomorrow we'll work on getting the IRS to back off for a while. I'll be home tomorrow afternoon."

"Good." She said nothing more, waiting. Katy swallowed a silent grin when she heard Garrett's next question.

"Miss me?"

"Yes, as a matter of fact, I do," she said demurely.

There was a pause and then Garrett said roughly, "I miss you, too. I'd much rather be climbing into bed with you than sitting here at this desk."

There was a voice in the background. It was a man's voice, and Katy listened attentively. "I take it you're not alone?"

"No, some of the staff are staying late with me. Did you and Emmett test that alarm system before the installer left? I couldn't hang around to check it out myself."

"Yes, we tested it. Works fine. We checked it out from both our house and the Brackens' place. Garrett, did you know Emmett keeps a gun in a cigar box right on top of the fireplace mantle? Emmett showed it to me this afternoon when we tested the alarm system."

"No, I didn't know, but it doesn't surprise me." There was a moment's silence. "Considering his drinking problem, I think the idea of him having a gun close at hand is not exactly reassuring, is it?"

"No, it isn't," Katy admitted. She wrapped her arms around her drawn-up knees. "I get the feeling he's the kind of drunk who just nods off to sleep, though, not the kind who gets violent."

"I don't know about those two, Katy. I hate to kick them out, but I'm not sure I want to keep them on forever, either. They were Atwood's concern, not ours."

"I know what you mean."

"Well, we'll talk about it when I get back. I've got enough on my mind this evening. Get some sleep, honey. I'll see you tomorrow."

Katy sighed as she hung up the phone. They hadn't exactly said good-night like lovers, but she had heard

the rough affection in his voice. Garrett did care for her.
She was sure of it. She had to be sure of it because she'd
staked her happiness on that assumption.

It was when she reached up to turn out the bedside
lamp that Katy saw the glint of gold in the small ceramic bowl on the dressing table. For a moment she
stared at it, wondering if she'd accidentally left some of
her jewelry out. Then she realized what it was.

Garrett had left his wedding ring behind before taking off for the Fresno office.

The optimism Katy had been feeling when she'd
climbed into bed a few minutes earlier faded. She got
up and walked slowly over to the dressing table. She
picked up the gold band and studied it with a feeling of
growing depression. The symbol of their marriage
meant so little to Garrett that he could casually take it
off and forget to put it back on.

Anger began to simmer in her. It seemed that every
time she thought she might be making progress in the
task of teaching Garrett how to love, something happened to puncture her balloon.

She thought of Garrett working late with his staff in
the Fresno office. He would be sitting at that desk, a
newly married man who wasn't even bothering to wear
a wedding ring.

Katy tugged the ring off her own finger and tossed it
down into the ceramic bowl beside Garrett's band.

The small gesture of getting even did little to make
her feel better.

THREE HOURS LATER Katy awoke with a surge of adrenaline. She sat bolt upright, aware of damp palms and a
trickle of perspiration under her arms. It took her a few

seconds to identify the shrill clamor that had awakened her so suddenly.

It was the new alarm system that had been rigged up on Red Dazzle's stall that afternoon.

Katy didn't stop to think. She threw off the covers and scrambled for her slippers. Grabbing her robe, she hurried down the hall, turning on lights as she went. She scurried downstairs, the robe flapping around her ankles. With any luck, whoever was fooling around the stables would soon realize he had awakened the inhabitants of the main house. The knowledge should send him scurrying.

Katy felt her ankle give way just as she reached the front steps. She grabbed the wrought-iron railing for support but knew it was too late. She had managed to twist the joint at its weak point. Pain shot through her. She set her teeth and forced herself to keep going. She would worry about the injury later.

Her slowed pace was maddening. With every step Katy bit back a groan. But she managed to half run, half hobble to the stable. A shadow loomed out of the darkness just as she reached the structure. Somehow Katy turned her scream into a shout. It was only a kid, she told herself. Only a troublemaking kid. Belatedly she realized how unarmed and vulnerable she was. She tried to compensate by putting as much authority as possible into her voice.

"Hey, you! Get away from there! Go on, get out of here before I call the police! This is private property!"

"Take it easy, Mrs. Coltrane—it's just me, Emmett Bracken."

Relief poured through Katy as the looming shadow took form and substance in the starlight. Emmett's voice was a little slurred, but he was obviously in control of himself.

"Emmett! Good grief, you gave me a scare. The new alarm went off up at the house. I thought someone was down here messing around with Red's stall door again." Katy sagged against a post, gasping for breath. Her ankle was throbbing violently.

"I woke up and couldn't get back to sleep. Thought I'd get some air to see if that would help. Came down to check on old Red, and I guess I set off the alarm by mistake. I promised your husband I'd keep an extra close eye on things while he was gone. I sure am sorry to upset you. Should have paid better attention this afternoon when that security man explained the alarm system. Are you all right, Mrs. Coltrane?" Emmett came toward her.

"I'm fine," Katy said through set teeth. "I may have sprained my ankle, but it will be okay." She looked around. The stable seemed peaceful enough. Limping painfully, she went inside and turned on the light.

Red Dazzle stirred sleepily and stuck his large head out over the stall door. He blinked owlishly at Katy, silently questioning the late-night ruckus.

Katy smiled and hobbled forward to stroke his neck. "Sorry about the rude awakening, Red. Go back to sleep."

The horse woofled grumpily and retreated into the dark shadows of his stall. A munching noise a few seconds later indicated he had decided that as long as he was up, he might as well have a midnight snack.

"Everything's fine," Emmett Bracken said, peering over Katy's shoulder into the stall. "Just a false alarm. Sure am sorry about all the excitement."

"That's okay, Emmett. I guess it takes a while to get accustomed to new alarm systems." Katy limped outside and turned out the stable light. "I'll see you in the morning."

"You want some help getting back to the house? That ankle of yours seems mighty weak."

"I can manage. This isn't the first time I've twisted it. Don't worry, I know exactly what to do for it." What she would do for it was suffer, Katy thought. She swore silently to herself and made her way slowly back to the main house.

So much for middle-of-the-night heroics. Something told her Garrett was going to blow his stack when he found out what had happened.

GARRETT DROVE BACK from Fresno with a feeling of pleasant anticipation. It took him a while to identify the unfamiliar sensation. He was accustomed to going back to an empty apartment. The idea of having a home of his own and a woman waiting for him seemed slightly unreal.

Not just a woman—a wife. His wife, Katy.

Garrett savored the notion of Katy waiting for him on the front steps with a welcoming drink in hand. It would be getting close to dinnertime, so she would probably have something interesting cooking in the kitchen. All in all, a man could do a whole lot worse.

After all his years of instability and change and uncertainty, permanence was amazingly good to think about.

The word *permanence* clanked loudly inside his head, striking a discordant note. A flicker of uneasiness invaded his pleasant sense of anticipation.

It suddenly occurred to him that even though things seemed to have settled down between himself and Katy, there was one issue that had not been discussed.

Neither of them had brought up the unpleasant matter of her initial agreement to stay with him for only three months.

Garrett's mouth tightened thoughtfully. Surely that nonsense was behind them now. Katy had capitulated completely two nights ago, after Hutton's party. She had given herself to him with all the sweet, sensual generosity of her spirit that night. She wasn't the type of woman who could surrender in that way unless she was totally committed, Garrett told himself.

But he had to face the fact that he was learning a lot of new things about Katy. She was a far more complex creature than he had originally thought. There was more to her, including a temper and a stubborn feminine will, than he had initially believed. He could no longer be completely certain of just what was going on inside her head.

His mind drifted back over the things she had said to him that night on the drive back from Hutton's cocktail party. There had been no mention of the three-month time limit. She had suggested only that they start sleeping together again because sleeping apart was too hard on both of them.

It was just barely conceivable that she had convinced herself she could have what amounted to nothing more than an affair with him for the remainder of the three months, Garrett realized.

His mood turned abruptly grim, and a cold wash of anger went through him. There were still some important matters to be resolved between himself and Katy.

Garrett wanted everything crystal clear between the two of them. Most of all, he wanted to be certain of her commitment to the marriage.

He remembered her flare of temper yesterday when he had informed her he was going to Fresno alone. Perhaps he should have taken her with him. But the truth was, he hadn't liked the idea of her talking about the business side of marriage when the honeymoon had just barely gotten off the ground. He had wanted her to accept her role as his wife before she got involved in her new job.

But he hadn't been able to think of a way to explain that to her, hadn't been at all sure she would accept the explanation, even if he had found the right words. So he had practically issued an order for her to stay behind while he went to Fresno.

Garrett swore. He had probably handled that scene all wrong yesterday. There was a hell of a lot to learn about handling a woman like Katy.

An hour later he turned into the long, tree-lined drive with a feeling of relief. He was home at last and Katy would be waiting. Tonight they would settle the last uncertainties that surrounded their marriage.

But Katy was not waiting on the front steps when Garrett finally parked the Mercedes and climbed out. Nor did she appear when he opened the front door and walked into the wide foyer. The house was very silent. Garrett felt himself tighten instinctively, as if he were preparing for a physical confrontation as he stalked up the stairs to the master bedroom. Deep in his guts, he sensed something was wrong.

The first thing that caught his eye as he threw open the bedroom door was the glint of gold in the ceramic dish on the dressing table. He flexed his left hand, belatedly realizing he had forgotten to put on his wedding ring yesterday morning after working around Red Dazzle's stall. He still wasn't accustomed to wearing the thing.

Then he saw the smaller, more delicate band of gold lying in the bowl alongside his own ring, and Garrett felt as if he'd been kicked in the stomach.

KATY SAT DOWN on a convenient boulder overlooking the ocean and absently rubbed her ankle. The breeze off the sea was turning from crisp and invigorating to blustery and threatening. Another storm was on the way.

Experimentally she rotated her foot. It was stiff but only mildly painful. Apparently she hadn't done as much damage as she had feared last night. Still, she admitted she probably shouldn't have attempted to walk along the cliffs after lunch. It had taken far longer than she had anticipated.

But she had gotten extremely bored sitting in Garrett's home waiting for his return. The decision to limp down to the cliffs overlooking the ocean had been an impulsive one that she was now regretting. She had justified it by telling herself she needed to work the ankle in order to keep it from stiffening up, but now she suspected she should have given it a full day of rest.

A month ago she wouldn't have been so impulsive, Katy acknowledged. Marriage to Garrett Coltrane was definitely having an effect on her normally placid, cautious, quiet ways. She wasn't certain if that effect was good or bad. The only thing she felt reasonably sure of was that the change was permanent. She didn't see herself ever sinking back into that quiet, serene, limited way of life she had lived for the past few years.

For better or worse, marriage had changed her. She could only hope Garrett was going through some changes, too.

The wind began to whine through the short, scruffy bushes that clung to the rocks along the cliffs. A dark, forbidding curtain stretched across the horizon, a herald of the storm to come. Katy clutched her jacket more tightly around her and got to her feet. It was time to start back to the house. At the rate she was moving today, it would take a while to make the journey.

Katy was in the process of turning back toward the path that led to the house when she spotted the dark figure standing some distance away, forlornly looking out to sea. At first she didn't recognize the person huddled into the old dark coat—then she saw the wind-tossed gray hair.

"Nadine!"

Katy started slowly toward the woman. There was no response, and she assumed Nadine hadn't heard her. The wind was getting forceful enough to obliterate the sound of a voice. Katy almost shrugged and gave up the attempt to call a greeting, but something stopped her. There was a look of such pathetic unhappiness about the dark figure on the cliffs that Katy couldn't bring herself to turn away. She moved laboriously closer to Nadine Bracken.

"Hi," she tried again as she approached the older woman. "That's some storm coming in, isn't it? It's getting cold and I think the first of the rain is about to hit. Want to walk back to the house together?"

At first Katy thought there was not going to be a response, but Nadine eventually turned her head. Katy was shocked by the expression she saw in the woman's eyes. The woman was staring at her as if Katy were a total stranger.

"Are you all right, Nadine?"

"Of course I'm all right." Nadine looked down at the water foaming at the base of the cliffs. "What are you doing out here?"

"Just thought I'd take a walk." Katy tried to keep her voice light and cheerful. She wasn't at all sure of Nadine Bracken's mood. Perhaps she was intruding. "I hurt my weak ankle last night, and I thought walking today might keep it from stiffening."

"What's wrong with your ankle?" Nadine seemed only remotely interested.

"I injured it badly a few years ago. If I push it too far these days, I'm asking for trouble. Last night I apparently overdid it when I went chasing down to Red Dazzle's stall."

Nadine looked at her with an unreadable gaze. "Emmett said the alarm went off accidentally."

Katy nodded. "I guess that's a problem with security systems. You have to learn to tolerate a few false alarms. They sure get the blood pumping, though."

There was silence on the cliffs for a few minutes. Again Katy almost made the decision to leave, but something held her. "It really is getting chilly out here, Nadine," she said gently. "Why don't you walk back with me? A cup of hot tea would taste great about now."

Nadine shook her head. "This is where it happened, you know," she said after a moment.

Katy eyed her curiously. "Where what happened?"

"This is where the boy was killed."

Katy glanced down at the treacherous cliff. "Silas Atwood's son? He died here?"

"That's right. He was down there on the beach, drinking with his friends. They had a party that night. Just a bunch of young kids. Big bonfire and too much alcohol. You know how teenagers are. No common sense. They started daring each other to climb up the cliff instead of using the path."

"In the dark?" Katy shivered as she looked down to the beach far below. The rock face was almost sheer. There were very few toeholds or clumps of weeds to grasp.

"Two of them made it. But when Brent Atwood tried it, he slipped on the rocks. Broke his neck."

"How terrible."

"It changed everything," Nadine whispered. "Everything. It wasn't right."

After a moment Nadine simply turned away without another word and started walking heavily back toward her cottage. Katy opened her mouth to call out to her but changed her mind when she saw the ramrod-stiff carriage of Nadine's chunky figure. The woman would not welcome any more conversation or companionship today. Katy felt a rush of sympathy, but she knew there was nothing she could do. Nadine had obviously been very attached to the Atwood family.

Slowly Katy made her way back toward the house. The rain reached land just as she was opening the kitchen door. The cup of tea she had offered Nadine sounded too good to pass up.

She was filling the tea kettle at the sink when she glanced outside and saw Garrett's car in the drive. He was home.

"Garrett?"

A mixture of emotions shot through her; chief among them was excitement. Katy put down the kettle and went into the living room. There was no sign of him. "Garrett? Where are you?" Perhaps he had gone to the stable to look in on Red Dazzle. She started up the stairs to see if his overnight case was in the bedroom.

She saw him standing beside the dressing table as she walked through the bedroom door. His eyes went to her face instantly as she came into the room. His right hand was closed in a fist. Katy had a rash impulse to throw herself into his arms. She risked a smile instead.

"Hello, Garrett. I didn't realize you were back. I was out on the cliffs, taking a walk. How was the drive?"

"The drive was fine." His voice sounded slightly hoarse and a little rusty, as if he wasn't quite certain how to use it. His amber eyes were glittering with an emotion Katy couldn't define. "There wasn't any problem until I got home and found this." He opened his hand, revealing the wedding rings.

Katy glanced warily at the gold bands cradled in his palm and suddenly realized she was on dangerous ground. Well, he had started this, she told herself. She kept her smile pinned firmly in place.

"Is something wrong, Garrett?"

"When I found your ring a minute ago, it crossed my mind that you had walked out on me while I was gone," he told her harshly.

Katy forced her smile up another notch. "As you can see, I haven't gone anywhere." She went forward and stood on tiptoe. Her mouth brushed lightly across his. Without giving him a chance to respond, she stepped back. "Are you hungry? I was going to put dinner on in a few minutes. How about a drink?"

"Dammit, Katy, I'm trying to talk to you."

"About what?" She looked at him innocently.

"About the fact that your wedding ring was sitting here on the dressing table," he retorted. "Mind explaining that?"

"What's to explain? Your ring was also sitting there. Why are you so upset, Garrett?"

"I told you why I'm upset. I thought you'd left."

"I haven't left," she repeated patiently.

"I can see that," he gritted. "What I want to know is why you took off your ring and put it here."

"It's simple enough, Garrett. I put my ring there because yours was there. Excuse me, I've got to go wash some lettuce for the salad."

He caught her before she got through the door. His hand closed around her shoulder and he spun her around to face him. "Katy, what kind of game are you playing with me?"

She shook her head. "I don't know what you're talking about."

"The hell you don't. Are you telling me you took off your wedding ring because you saw that I'd left mine behind?"

Katy summoned up another smile. "We both want this marriage to be on a totally equal footing, don't we?"

Sheer, unadulterated masculine outrage blazed in his eyes. "Now you listen to me, lady, and you listen good. I took off my ring to work around the stables yesterday morning. It's dangerous to wear a ring when you're working with tools. When I set out for Fresno, I was in a hurry, as you well know. I'd been busy until the last minute with the alarm system guy, remember? I threw some clothes in a bag and went. I forgot to put the ring back on, that's all."

"Maybe next time you'll remember," Katy murmured. She ducked out from under his hand and tried once more to escape.

"Why, you little witch." He caught her again, this time anchoring her with both hands on her shoulders as he forced her to confront him. "What the devil did you think you were going to accomplish?" His eyes narrowed as he glowered down at her. And then realization dawned in his eyes. "You were trying to teach me a lesson, weren't you?"

"Actually," Katy admitted judiciously, "when I first saw your ring lying there last night, I had just hung up the phone from talking to you. I realized you were over there in beautiful downtown Fresno, working late with your staff and that you would probably have a drink with everyone later when the job was done. They would all know about your recent marriage, of course, and they would all probably look for your new ring. I wondered what they would be thinking when they realized you weren't wearing it."

"Nobody but a woman would put together a scenario like that!" Garrett roared.

"In case it's escaped your notice, I am a woman."

Garrett's expression turned even more fierce. "Don't get sassy with me, Katy."

"I'm not being sassy. I'm being assertive." Katy tried to step clear of him. His hands didn't give an inch. She was locked in place.

"I think I'm finally beginning to put this all together. You were really upset, weren't you? You thought I had left my ring behind deliberately and you decided to get even."

Katy considered that carefully. "Let's just say I was annoyed that you found it so easy to forget to wear your ring. It made me wonder just how casually you regarded our marriage."

Garrett gave her a slight shake, but to her amazement he was no longer glaring at her. Instead there was the suspicious hint of a smile in his eyes. His mouth curved faintly as he studied her face.

"You know damned well I don't regard it in a casual light," he said.

"Well, you can't blame me for getting that impression," she retorted.

"Sure I can and I do. You know me better than that, Katy. I'm a married man, whether I remember to wear my ring or not." There was an undertone of unyielding pride in the words. "I don't take my responsibilities as a husband lightly."

Katy sensed the strength of that unbending, arrogant pride, and something in her relaxed. She drew a deep breath. "I believe you. If it makes you feel any better, I consider myself thoroughly married, too, even if I happen not to be wearing my ring."

They stared at each other for a long moment, each clearly sizing up the other. Then Garrett pulled Katy abruptly against him. His arms went around her in a tight, compelling embrace.

"I'm glad you consider yourself thoroughly married because you are thoroughly married. So am I."

Katy swallowed back the wave of emotion that poured through her. She put her arms around Garrett's waist and leaned heavily into his strength. "Welcome home, Garrett."

He chuckled into her hair. "Thanks. But do me a favor the next time I come home after a business trip. Don't spring any surprises on me like this one. I'm not sure I can take the shock."

Katy lifted her head. "Was it really a shock to see my ring lying there beside yours?"

He tangled his hands in her hair and kissed her with rough passion. "Let's just say you made your point. I'm not likely to forget to put my ring on next time when I leave the house."

"Good."

Garrett laughed at the depth of satisfaction in her voice. He tumbled her down onto the bed and sprawled on top of her. Very deliberately he caught her hand and slipped her wedding ring back on her finger. "You are turning out to be one surprise after another, Katy Coltrane. Who would have thought you had such a streak of primitive female pride in you? You always seemed so . . . so . . ."

"Sensible? Calm? Rational? Demure? Level-headed?"

Garrett grinned wickedly, putting on his own ring. Then his fingers went to the buttons of Katy's shirt. "Yeah. Something like that."

"Garrett, what about dinner?"

"We can eat later. Right now I've got other things on my mind."

"I noticed." Katy sighed happily and started to work on the buttons of his shirt.

## 9

"SPEAKING OF SHOCKS," Katy began an hour and a half later as she and Garrett finally sat down to dinner, "I had a mild one myself last night around midnight."

Garrett looked up from his salmon and fettucine. His eyes, which had been full of lazy contentment since the lovemaking in the bedroom, suddenly gleamed with alertness. "What happened?"

"Emmett accidentally tripped the new alarm on Red Dazzle's stall. I went down to check it out." Katy went on to explain the events of the night. "It seems to be a very sensitive system," she concluded.

"It's supposed to be sensitive." Garrett dismissed that fact impatiently and glared at Katy. "What the devil did you think you were doing dashing off in response to it, though? It was the middle of the night. It could have been anyone down there at the stable, a young punk, a dangerous vagrant, *anyone*."

Katy sighed inwardly and picked up her wineglass. She had been afraid of this. "Calm down, Garrett. Nothing happened. I told you, it was just an accident."

Garrett was not so easily placated. "That was a stupid thing to do, Katy. You should have called Emmett's cottage or called the cops, but you sure as hell had no business chasing down to the stable by yourself."

"Garrett—"

"I'm not through yet," he informed her. He planted both elbows on the table and proceeded to chew her out thoroughly for another five minutes on the subject of reckless, impulsive behavior. The salmon and fettucine got cold.

Her husband had a distinct talent for making his feelings known on such matters, Katy decided. He might not be able to tell her that he loved her, but he certainly had no problem telling her he was annoyed with her. Katy waited until he finally wound down and then she smiled hopefully. "Now are you through?"

"You're not taking me seriously, are you?"

Katy nodded quickly. "Yes, I am, I promise. I know I reacted hastily last night, but everything turned out all right and I really don't need the lecture today. Tell me about your trip to Fresno, instead."

Garrett muttered a dark warning about never doing such a thing again and then gave up the thankless job of taking his wife to task for her foolishness. He poured himself another glass of wine.

"The trip was reasonably successful. We salvaged the Bisbys for a while, at any rate. A classic case of hard work and bad management. All the back-breaking, dawn-to-dusk work in the world won't do a farmer or a rancher a damned bit of good if he doesn't have a handle on the management and accounting end of things. Management and planning are everything. In this day and age, the only ones that are going to make it are the ones who know how to run cattle and crops like a real business. The Bisbys of this world are just like my father. They pour everything they have into the land but nothing into learning about the business of managing it."

"Your father didn't have Coltrane and Company to call on for advice and assistance," Katy pointed out softly.

"Knowing my father, I'd say he probably wouldn't have listened, even if help had been offered. He was an old-fashioned rancher who thought he knew all there was to know about cattle. It wouldn't have occurred to him that he could have used some management consulting. So he wound up losing the two things that mattered the most to him—his land and his woman. After that he didn't have much to live for, I guess." Garrett stabbed at his food with subdued violence.

Katy ate slowly, thinking about what that loss had meant. Garrett's father had died in a senseless one-car accident on a county road when Garrett was in his teens. Some had suspected suicide. Some had suspected drunk driving. It was shortly after that Harry Randall, who had known the Coltrane family for years, had given Garrett the stable job.

The only steady thing in Garrett's life had been his part-time job in the Randall stables. Later, when he had learned he could make a lot more money on the rodeo circuit, Garrett had quit his job. Harry Randall had understood and wished him well.

Garrett was finishing the last of his meal when he surprised Katy with an announcement.

"I thought I'd invite some friends over next Friday evening." He watched Katy's face as he spoke. "Bob and Diane Greeley. Bob's an old rodeo hand. He and I used to hang out together on the circuit. Roped as a team. You'll like Diane."

Katy nodded acquiescently. "Is Bob still on the circuit?"

"Nope. Like me, he got smart and got out before he broke every bone in his body. He went back to college and got a degree in computer science, of all things."

Katy smiled. "Hard to imagine a rodeo cowboy becoming a computer expert."

Garrett didn't return the smile. "I know what you classy show-ring types think about cowboys. It's probably hard for you to believe they're capable of thinking about anything more refined than bulls, beer and broads."

Katy raised her eyebrows. "If I ever did have such limited notions, you've certainly set me straight, haven't you? You've come a long way from the rodeo circuit."

Garrett relaxed, his mouth crooking ruefully. "Sorry. Didn't mean to jump all over you. Sometimes the old feelings resurface."

*And sometimes, the old feelings never quite fade away,* Katy thought with a flash of insight.

"Get Nadine to help you with dinner on Friday night," Garrett said. "No reason you should knock yourself out. I want you to enjoy the evening. I think you and Diane will hit it off."

Katy nodded, realizing from the way he said it that he really wanted her and the unknown Diane to be friends. Garrett was trying to provide her with a friend in the area, one more inducement to settle down and be contented with her lot as his wife. It was a touching thought.

INVOLVING NADINE BRACKEN in the Friday-evening dinner preparations proved unexpectedly difficult. Katy sat down with the older woman on Thursday to go over the menu. She went through her plans for paella, salad and sourdough bread.

"I thought we could have cheese wafers, smoked oysters in pastry and fresh vegetables together with a sour cream dip, for hors d'oeuvres," Katy concluded. "None of this is too complicated. The preparation can all be taken care of ahead of time."

Nadine glared at the menu for a long moment and then finally announced, "Mrs. Atwood never served anything like this paella to her guests. She always served the best cut of steaks. Mr. Atwood cooked them on the barbecue out back. He enjoyed doing that."

Katy blinked. "Ah, yes, well, I prefer seafood to steaks so I think we'll go with the paella. I'd also like to have a cheesecake for dessert."

"It just won't be the same," Nadine warned.

Katy smiled coolly. "No," she agreed, "it won't be the same."

"I don't know why things have to keep changing," Nadine muttered as she got to her feet. "I just don't know why."

Katy sighed and wondered privately if it wouldn't be easier to take care of the Friday-night dinner preparations by herself. She liked to cook and the truth was, she was only involving Nadine because Garrett had wanted her to do so.

The next three days passed without incident. Garrett busied himself with small chores around the stables and the house. As far as business went, he contented himself with daily phone calls to his office. He took Katy to San Luis Obispo for shopping and sight-seeing, and they stopped by the college campus to visit one of Garrett's friends on the faculty.

During the days, Katy was aware of Garrett watching her closely. She felt as if everything she said or did was being monitored to see if she showed evidence of settling down permanently into the role of wife. At times it was very unnerving. At other times Katy tried to assure herself it was a good sign.

At night Garrett made love to her with a passion and urgency that left no doubt that he was not above using sex to try to bind her to him. He would hold back, keeping himself savagely in check until she cried out and convulsed gently in his arms. Only then would he sink himself into her completely and take his own satisfaction.

On Thursday morning Katy surprised Garrett in his study in the act of concluding a phone call. She had just opened the door to see if he was around, and his reaction startled her. He had finished the call with a brusque farewell.

"You know what I want. Everything's arranged on this end. Just be sure everything's taken care of at your end. I'll talk to you later." Garrett had replaced the phone abruptly, swiveling around in his chair to confront Katy. He scowled at her. "What is it, Katy?"

"Nothing. I was going to go for a walk on the cliffs. I wondered if you wanted to join me. But if you're busy we'll make it later."

"No." He got to his feet, reaching for his Stetson. "I could use a little exercise. Let's go." He had hustled her out of the room as if anxious to get her away from the scene of the phone call.

Katy toyed with the idea of demanding an explanation but something stopped her. She sensed instinctively Garrett would not appreciate being pinned down about the mysterious phone call. She decided to let it ride. There were still many areas in which she felt obliged to tread cautiously around her new husband.

She took consolation in the fact that he still apparently felt obliged to walk carefully around her, too. It was an interesting, if occasionally unsettling, situation. She wondered frequently if it would lead to love.

FRIDAY EVENING arrived and began to unfold without incident, in spite of Nadine Bracken's reluctance to condone paella as a fitting meal to be served in the old Atwood home.

Garrett had been secretly amused by the small domestic confrontation between his wife and Nadine. If Nadine had thought she could dominate the new young lady of the house, she'd learned the truth now. Katy might come across initially as gentle and sweet and shy and manipulable but the fact was, there was a stubborn will buried under all that softness. Garrett himself had recently had a few lessons on the subject, and it gave him a certain amount of satisfaction to see someone else undergoing the same education.

It also pleased him to see Katy asserting herself in her own house. It meant she might be finally starting to think of it as her real home.

For the past few days he had been watching Katy intently for signs of progress. She was everything he could want in bed, and during the day she seemed happy to be a wife.

But the raw fact he kept chewing on was that the three-month deadline she had originally set on the marriage had never been officially lifted. The knowledge that Katy might still be thinking of leaving after three short months was a constant goad. More than once Garrett had been strongly tempted to bring the subject out into the open and demand that Katy admit she was no longer thinking of their marriage as a three-month-long affair. But inevitably he'd talked himself out of the showdown.

It wasn't like him to let something this serious stay under wraps. He was a man accustomed to facing life and forcing it into the path he wanted. But he wasn't altogether certain how to go about forcing Katy into the role of committed wife.

At five o'clock Katy came into the master bedroom to dress. Garrett was just finishing his shower. He saw her as he came out of the bathroom.

"Everything all set for dinner?" he asked.

"I think so. We'll eat around seven-thirty." Katy started into the still-steamy bathroom, unbuttoning her blouse as she went. She was still shy around him, and Garrett knew she would finish undressing behind the closed door of the bathroom. It was ridiculous. This same woman would catch fire in his arms later that night when he made love to her. She wouldn't be at all shy then. She would be hungry and exciting and full of soft, feminine, passionate demand. She would ride him the way she had once ridden her father's magnificent Arabians and he would lose himself in her.

And if she thought she could give him that for three months and then call it quits, she had another think coming. With sudden resolve, Garrett took a step forward.

"Katy."

The rough edge in his voice stopped her abruptly. She glanced back inquiringly over her shoulder. "Yes, Garrett?"

He folded his arms and leaned against the closet door, studying her. His whole body was throbbing with an urgent need to nail down his future with Katy.

"I want to talk to you," he said in a voice that was as neutral as he could manage.

"About what?"

"About your plans for the future."

"My plans?" She tilted her head and regarded him curiously. "What about them?"

"I have a right to know what you think you're going to do at the end of three months, Katy. I want to know if you still plan to walk away from our marriage."

She stared at him, her gray eyes unfathomable. It was rare that she could succeed in hiding her thoughts from him, Garrett realized. Usually he could read what she was thinking just by looking into those huge cloud-colored pools. But not tonight.

"Garrett, this is hardly the time to discuss our marriage. We've got guests coming in less than an hour and I'm not even dressed."

"You're still thinking of running away from me after three months, aren't you?" he challenged.

She edged toward the bathroom door, clutching her unbuttoned blouse across her breasts. "You make me sound like a teenage bride who's planning on running home to mama. That's hardly the case. If things end after three months I'm sure we'll both handle the...the dissolution of our marriage in a mature, adult, businesslike manner. Neither of us is a child."

Garrett felt a violent tension ripple through his whole body. She was still thinking of leaving him.

He could hardly believe it. She had appeared to be settling down. She was looking forward to starting work in his office, and he knew he was satisfying her at night. What more could a woman want, he demanded silently of the universe. Instantly his mind shied away from the answer she had given him the morning after the wedding. Instead he opted for the approach that had always served him well in a world that was constantly shifting underfoot. It was time to flex a little muscle.

Garrett didn't move. He stayed where he was against the closet door and pinned Katy with his eyes. "What makes you think I'll let you act as if you're involved in nothing more than an affair for three months, Katy?"

She took another step toward the bathroom. "Calm down, Garrett. There's no need to become irrational about this."

"I'm not the one who's behaving irrationally. You're the fluff-headed little fool who thinks she's got a legitimate gripe just because marriage didn't prove to be the romantic hearts-and-flowers arrangement she'd fantasized about."

"Take it easy, Garrett. Your guests will be here soon, and I've got a lot to do." She was safely over the bathroom threshold now, reaching for the door.

Garrett came away from the closet. He started forward with slow, deliberate strides. It was like dealing with a fractious little mare, he told himself. If he moved too quickly, she would turn tail and run. If he didn't move at all, she would think she had won the encounter and she would be even more difficult to handle later.

"I don't know where you got your notions of what marriage is supposed to be all about, Katy, but I think it's time somebody set you straight. Who better to do that than your husband? I'll tell you what marriage is about. It's about sticking it out when the going gets tough or the money gets short. It's about honoring the promises you made in front of witnesses. It's about building something lasting. It's about commitment. If you think I'm going to let you run away from that commitment, you'd better think again. I'm putting you on notice, lady. There's no place on this earth where you can hide that I can't find you. If it comes down to the crunch, I'm a lot stronger, tougher and meaner than you'll ever be. Remember that."

"I don't need lectures on the subject of marriage from you, dammit!"

Katy jumped back and slammed the bathroom door in Garrett's face. A split second later he heard the lock click. Swearing softly, he slammed the wooden door frame with his open palm, turned around and went back to the closet to finish dressing. He winced as he yanked his trousers off the hanger. His hand hurt.

GARRETT HAD BEEN RIGHT about one thing, Katy decided later that evening—she did, indeed, like Diane Greeley. The other woman was small, petite and blond. She was not a raving beauty, but she had a lovely smile and warm blue eyes. Diane was also very pregnant.

"Seven months," Diane confided as she followed Katy on a tour of the house. "Bob and I can hardly wait. We put it off so long while Bob went back to college that we both began to worry." She glanced around at the interior of the huge home. "Looks like you and Garrett had better get busy, too, if you want to fill this place up with kids."

Katy smiled whimsically, seeing the house through Diane's eyes. She decided not to mention the fact that Garrett had never brought up the subject of children. "It really is a lot of house, isn't it?"

Diane chuckled. "I knew that when he finally bought a home of his own, Garrett would do it in a big way. He always makes his plans very carefully, like a good general going into battle. And he never acts until he's absolutely sure of what he's doing. Garrett always seems to have everything under control, doesn't he?"

*Everything except me,* Katy thought, remembering the short, fiery exchange in the bedroom before Diane and Bob arrived. She felt a twinge of unease when she realized that in a few more hours she would be alone with Garrett once more. It didn't take any great amount of wifely intuition to know that he did not consider the argument concluded.

"Have you known Garrett a long time?" Diane asked as the two women walked slowly toward the staircase.

"I knew him when I was a kid. But he left town when I was twelve, and I didn't see much of him again until a few months ago," Katy said.

Diane nodded. "Bob told me something about Garrett's background once. Sounds like it was rather rough."

"It was."

"I heard his parents lost the family ranch and that Garrett's mother left." Diane slanted Katy a curious glance. "Garrett grew up more or less on his own after that, I gather?"

"More or less. He started out on the rodeo circuit when he left high school."

Diane laughed, shaking her head. "Talk about replacing one insecure life-style with another equally uncertain one. That rodeo business is enough to drive any person to drink. A man is constantly on the move to the next town. His family life is usually a disaster. He has no financial security at all and he never knows whether the next fall he takes is going to kill him or just break a couple of bones." Diane shuddered. "There's never any security. I can't tell you how glad I am that Bob got out when he did. I know you must be equally glad Garrett had the intelligence and the determination to do the same. So many of those cowboys don't. Of course that left both Bob and Garrett with the job of building whole new careers."

*Never any security.*

Something clicked in Katy's mind as Diane's words sank in. For most of his life Garrett had never known any stability or security except that which he had forged for himself. He had learned long ago not to rely on anyone. She had known that all along, but it was only now that the full implications of the knowledge struck home. She stopped at the top of the stairs and turned to stare at her new friend.

"Is something wrong?" Diane asked, alarmed.

"No." Katy shook her head slowly. "No. Nothing's wrong. I just realized I've been looking at something backward."

It was Diane's turn to stare. "Backward?"

"Yes. Upside down and backward."

"Uh, was it something I said?" Diane asked warily.

Katy laughed softly. "Yes, as a matter of fact, it was. I should have seen it for myself but I've been paying too much attention to my own feelings. I didn't stop to realize—" She broke off. "Never mind. I must sound like my mind is wandering. Let's go downstairs and join the men. They're probably nearing starvation."

Garrett looked up from Bob Greeley, who had been talking, just as Katy came down the stairs alongside Diane. His eyes met hers, and Katy trembled for an instant at the expression she saw in his golden gaze. He wanted her. He would do whatever he had to do in order to hold on to her. For Garrett, that constituted love.

She should have understood, Katy told herself. She should have realized she was making a gigantic mistake when she had threatened to pull the rug out from under Garrett. He was accustomed to having it pulled out from under him. By holding the three-month time limit over his head she had been doing to him what everything and everyone had always done to him. She had been telling him he couldn't count on her or her love.

It was suddenly very important that Garrett realize he could depend on her love.

Then Bob moved forward to hand his wife a glass of fruit juice and the small spell was broken. Bob was a tall, rangy man with laughing brown eyes and a ready smile. "Quite a house, isn't it, honey?" he asked. "I was just telling Garrett here that he's come a long way from those fleabag motels on the rodeo circuit."

"So have you," Diane pointed out affectionately. She smiled at Katy. "I was just saying to Katy that she and Garrett were going to have to get busy and fill up this place with kids. A big house like this needs a family."

Aware that Garrett was watching her more closely than ever, Katy felt a rush of color sweep into her cheeks. "If you'll excuse me, I'll go check with Nadine. The paella should be about ready." Katy was glad to be able to make even a temporary escape. She had a lot to think about.

Three hours later Katy again found herself alone with her husband. Ever since the conversation with Diane she had been thinking of ways to handle the coming scene with Garrett. But her mind felt jumbled and unclear. She didn't know whether to blurt out her intention to stay and make the marriage work or to lead up to it in a more mature, sophisticated, subtle fashion. She wasn't at all sure there was a more mature, sophisticated or subtle way to do it. It all seemed fairly raw and basic. She decided to try for the middle ground.

"Things went well, didn't they?" Katy remarked on the way up the stairs. "I enjoyed meeting Diane and Bob."

Garrett said nothing. He unfastened the cuffs of his shirt as he climbed the stairs beside Katy. All his attention appeared focused on the task.

"I was worried Nadine might decide to sabotage the paella, but she didn't," Katy went on with determined cheerfulness. "Everything came through just fine, including the cheesecake."

Garrett still said nothing. They were walking down the hall to the bedroom now. Katy began to grow more nervous. She took a deep breath as she stepped through the bedroom door. "Garrett . . ."

He closed the door with a soft finality and leaned back against it, facing her. His expression was harsh.

"Have you considered the fact that you might be pregnant?" he asked.

Katy nearly choked. She thought of the little pills she had been taking for a few weeks. "Uh, no, I haven't. It's not possible. I went to the doctor before we were married. I've been taking the pill."

"I see." He continued to regard her in silence.

Katy grew flustered. This wasn't going at all the way she had planned. "Garrett, I would like to talk to you about, well, about what we were, uh, discussing earlier this evening."

He ignored that, his eyes gravely serious. "I would be a good father, Katy. I know you probably don't think so because of the way my own father was, but that's just the reason why I would be a good one. Do you understand? I'd take care of my family. You don't have to be afraid that I'd leave you and the kid alone. You could trust me, Katy."

Emotion nearly overwhelmed her. "I do trust you," she whispered. "If you say you'll stick around, I'll believe you."

"I've already said I'll stick around. I said that much on our wedding day when I took those vows, remember?"

"I remember."

"You're the one who's been waffling, lady. Not me."

"I know. I'm sorry." She walked slowly toward him, her smile tremulous. "I had it all wrong."

He scowled at her. "Had what all wrong?"

"Never mind. It's time you knew that I plan to stick around, too. I won't be going anywhere after three months, Garrett. Not unless you ask me to leave." She laced her arms around his neck.

Incredulous relief and satisfaction flared in his eyes. "*Katy*. It's about time, you admitted that. It's about time."

He picked her up and carried her to the bed. He began to undress her with such tenderness, such exquisite care, that Katy almost cried. Instead she reached for him and drew him down on her. Her fingers trembled as she began undoing the buttons of his shirt.

"Katy, my sweet little Katy." Garrett's voice was husky with emotion. "Everything's going to be all right now."

"Yes, Garrett. Everything's going to be all right."

He finished undressing her and when she was lying nude beside him, Garrett lifted himself up on one elbow to gaze hungrily down at Katy. His hand moved over her with gentle possession. He touched her breasts, drawing tiny, exciting circles around each nipple until both responded by forming small, hard peaks.

Garrett leaned down to taste the tips of Katy's breasts. As he did so he caught one of her questioning hands and guided her fingers to his strong, thrusting shaft. When her palm closed around him he groaned with an aching pleasure.

Katy teased him gently, delighting in the sweet, feminine power she had over him. Then she felt his fingers in the silken hair between her legs and she cried out softly.

Garrett's dark head bent over her as he worked a string of kisses slowly down the length of her body. When he parted her with his fingers and kissed the soft, vulnerable flesh of her inner thighs, Katy gasped.

And then her fingers were digging into him and Garrett was settling himself within the cradle of her legs.

She clung to him as he pushed powerfully forward, entering her with a harsh exclamation of satisfaction.

"Hold me," Garret whispered thickly. "Hold me, Katy."

She held him as if her whole future depended on it.

# 10

GARRETT SPENT THE WEEKEND basking in the many and assorted pleasures of being a happily married man. There were, he was discovering, a host of advantages, not the least of which was a comfortable feeling of rightness.

"You don't know what you're missing, Red," he told the gelding on Monday morning.

Red Dazzle, who had been attempting to take his morning nap, blinked sleepily and ambled over to the paddock fence. Garrett laughed softly and patted the horse's neck. Red dozed contentedly in the morning sunshine.

"She's finally settled down," Garrett told the horse. "No more talk about three-month deadlines and no more nasty cracks about our 'business partnership.' It's been a rough honeymoon, but I think we've finally got everything ironed out. Who would have thought one little female would have packed so much sheer cussed stubbornness?"

Red Dazzle declined to answer.

"She loves me, you know," Garrett explained. "She had a crush on me when she was just a kid, and now she's a full-grown woman and she's in love with me. She told me on our wedding night."

But she hadn't repeated the confession since that disastrous evening, Garrett admitted silently. It was the

only thing that was still bothering him. Katy had surrendered all her bristling defenses except the last one.

It hadn't even dawned on Garrett that there was still
one more barrier to demolish, until he had awakened
that morning and realized Katy had not repeated her
wedding night confession of love.

It shouldn't bother him. He had everything else he
wanted and needed from her, he told himself. She had
committed herself to the marriage at last. She had even
told him she would trust him to be a good father for
their children.

That admission had shaken him. It wasn't until she
had made it that he had realized how important it was
to him to hear her talk about children. When he had
seen how pregnant Diane Greeley was on Friday night,
all Garrett had been able to think about was what Katy
would look like carrying his child. He had spent most
of the evening envisioning her all soft and round with
his baby.

Then he had acknowledged that Katy might have
several reservations about making a baby with a man
who had grown up with a very limited home life. The
thought that she might not want his child had sent a
cold chill through Garrett. It was a subject he had not
even thought about before the wedding except in the
vaguest of terms. He took it for granted that eventually there would be children. Children were pieces of
the future, and he fully intended to ensure that part of
his future. But on Friday night the subject was no longer
a vague, distant one. It had suddenly dominated his
whole world. He could still feel the incredible relief he
had experienced when Katy had assured him she would
trust him to be a father.

That relief coupled with her willingness to abandon the three-month time limit on the marriage had satisfied him for the remainder of the weekend. He and Katy had spent much of the time playing like the lovers they were.

It was only this morning that Garrett realized there was one more small, niggling, but surprisingly important hurdle left. He wanted to hear Katy tell him she loved him again. He wanted to hear the soft, sweet words he had heard on his wedding night.

"No doubt about it, Red, I've turned into a greedy man." Garrett gave the gelding one last affectionate slap. "Well, I'd better check your new roommate's quarters. Wouldn't want the little lady to be shocked. You know how these gently bred, cosseted females are. They don't take kindly to the idea of roughing it. Got to handle 'em with kid gloves."

The way he had been handling Katy, Garrett told himself as he strode into the stables. Katy had a lot in common with the delicate Arabian mare that would be arriving that afternoon. Spirited but gentle. Both needed a light hand on the reins. The last thing Garrett wanted to do was bruise either one of them. But he also had no intention of losing either one.

The mare was going to be a surprise for Katy, a surprise Garrett was realistic enough to admit she might not be exactly thrilled with at the start. But he was complacently optimistic. Some people didn't know what was good for them at first sight, but they could learn. He was convinced that eventually Katy would thank him for what he was about to do. He was going to get her back into riding and when she rediscovered the joy she had once known, she would turn to him with gratitude in her eyes.

Gratitude and love.

He had ordered the three-year-old Arabian from Harry Randall last week and finalized the arrangements in a phone call that Katy had unwittingly interrupted. The animal was due to be delivered today.

KATY WAS FINALLY BEGINNING to enjoy her honeymoon. It had been a strange period of time, filled with highs and lows and unexpected curves, but she was feeling more serene now than she had at any point since her wedding day. As honeymoons went, this one had hardly been idyllic, but there was no doubt that she had learned a great deal about her new husband.

She had also learned something about herself.

As she walked from the house to the stables, Katy thought about those personal discoveries. She had never dreamed she would turn out to be the type of woman who could be overcome with passion, for example. She had a hunch Garrett had been equally astonished, though he'd been far too gallant to comment on the subject.

She had also never thought of herself as stubborn, temperamental or demanding, either. But during the past several days she had learned she was capable of indulging all those interesting human traits and a few others, as well.

Katy was smiling secretly when she reached the stables.

"Garrett? Where are you?"

"In here."

She followed the sound of his voice through the stable door. He was checking the hardware on the empty stall next to Red Dazzle's. "What are you doing?"

"Just going over a few things," he explained cryptically.

"Oh. You've been spending a lot of time down here at the stables lately. Is everything all right with the alarm system?"

"Everything's fine," he assured her. He emerged from the stall, a lazy, affectionate grin on his face. He shoved his hat back on his head. "I could use a cup of coffee, though. How about you?" He reached out to snag her hand and hold on to it.

"Sure. We really should do some grocery shopping today. I wouldn't mind investigating a few of those little dress shops you pointed out the other day. Diane gave me some names of the ones she likes. And it's about time you showed me your main offices."

"We've got plenty of time for you to learn about Coltrane and Company," Garrett said dismissively. "Let's not rush things. I'm still enjoying the honeymoon."

"Is that right?" she teased. "What about that talk you have to give this evening to that group of cattlemen? Is that any way to spend one of your honeymoon evenings?"

Garrett groaned. "Don't remind me. I made that commitment a couple of months ago and there's no way I can get out of it. I'll only be gone a few hours. I should be home by nine o'clock at the latest."

"I could go with you," Katy suggested.

"I've told you, honey, this is an all-male group. You'd feel out of place, and I'd spend the whole evening fighting off lecherous cattlemen."

"Bunch of chauvinists, I take it?"

"When you're talking ranchers and farmers, you're talking old-fashioned, unenlightened males," Garrett agreed blandly.

"What about you?" Katy laughed up at him with her eyes. "Are you in that old-fashioned, unenlightened category?"

"Of course not." Garrett's tone was one of lofty arrogance. "I'm one of the new breed—haven't you noticed? Hell, I'm even going to make my wife a partner in my business. What more proof do you need of my enlightened ways?"

"I'm not so sure making me a partner qualifies as an example of your advanced thinking and attitudes. It could be just a way of getting free work out of me."

Garrett contrived to look hurt. "I'm crushed."

"Uh-huh." Katy was humorously skeptical. "You know what I think? I think that deep down you are one very old-fashioned—" She broke off at the sound of a vehicle in the driveway. "Were we expecting anyone?" she asked as she turned to glance behind her.

Garrett stopped and draped his arm around her shoulders. He watched the truck and horse trailer approaching, his expression one of quiet expectation. "We," he announced cheerfully, "are expecting a new stablemate for Red Dazzle. You're going to love her."

"What on earth are you talking about?" Katy stared at the horse trailer as the truck came to a halt. "Did you buy another horse for yourself?"

"Not for me, although I'll admit I've got my eye on a good-looking young stallion your father is trying to sell me. But this little lady is for you." Garrett started forward, dragging Katy easily along with him. "Her name is Shadow Silk. Remember her?"

"Shadow Silk! That's one of my father's mares!" Katy groped for an explanation, panicked by the one that was taking shape. "What do you mean, she's for me? Garrett, what have you done?"

"I bought her for you," he said simply. His arm tightened slightly around her shoulders as if he expected her to pull away. "Relax, honey. We'll take it slow and easy."

"Take what slow and easy?" Katy felt a flame of wild anger spring to life within her as she realized just what Garrett had in mind. "If you think you can force me back on a horse, you're out of your mind. How dare you pull a trick like this! How dare you? Who do you think you are, Garrett Coltrane?"

"Calm down. Just take it easy, honey. Everything's going to be okay."

"Don't talk to me as if I were a horse, dammit!" Katy felt her voice crawling up the scale toward hysteria. Frantically she struggled for self-control. Her throat was suddenly tight with intense emotion. "Garrett, you had no right to spring this on me. You can send Shadow Silk back to my father right now, do you hear me?"

"I hear you. So does the driver of the truck and anyone else within shouting distance." Garrett's tone lost a measure of its soothing quality. It was replaced by an implacable firmness. "I hate to have to be the one to point this out to you, but you're making a scene and you know how you hate scenes. Now why don't you just calm down and let me see about getting your new mare unloaded and into her stall."

Tears of fury and frustration were stinging Katy's eyes. Her hands clenched into small fists. Her breath felt tight in her chest. She wanted to scream and couldn't get the words out. "You don't understand," she managed in a strangled whisper. "You just don't understand. No one does. Even my parents and my friends never understood, not really. Why can't any of you just accept my right to make my own decisions? I don't ever want to ride a horse again as long as I live. How much clearer can I make it?"

Garrett frowned, catching her face between rough palms. "Honey, it's time you got over your fear. Riding was once the most important thing in your life. You loved it. You're going to love it again. We're going to ride together a lot, you and I. It's going to be one of the things we share."

Despairingly Katy shook her head, knowing she did not have the words to make him comprehend her fear. "You just don't understand."

"I know what it's like to be afraid, honey," he surprised her by saying. "I also know that the only solution is to face the fear. You should have gotten back up on a horse years ago."

"I chose not to ride again!"

"Well, someone should have overridden your decision."

"Is that what you think you're going to succeed in doing now?" she challenged.

"It's what I know I'm going to succeed in doing."

"Not a chance, Garrett. Do you hear me? Not a chance!" Katy turned and started toward the house. She refused to look back. The anger in her was unlike anything she had ever known.

It was, amazingly enough, even stronger than the fear.

A few minutes later she watched through the kitchen window as Shadow Silk was untrailered and led into the stable. Katy remembered the small, delicate mare well. Shadow Silk was a lovely creature, full of grace and equine power. The mare was a dappled gray with a dark, high-arched tail and a dark mane. Her conformation was excellent, a good, deep chest, a refined head, a short back. The mare was a fine example of the excellent breeding program at Randall Farm. She had a fine pedigree. Katy could recite that pedigree back for generations. She also knew that the mare was beautifully trained, with a soft mouth and a good disposition. All her father's animals were trained with patience and gentleness.

But even the most even-tempered horse turned dangerous when it was panicked, and even the most perfectly trained animal became a lunging, thirteen-hundred-pound juggernaut of flashing hooves when it was caught in the grip of terror. A 115-pound human being was no match for such a creature. Katy shivered as memories swept through her.

Those memories had been sufficiently unnerving to keep Katy from getting back on a horse for several years. For a while her parents and others had urged her to try riding again, but in the end her quiet resistance had defeated them. No one had wanted to pressure her too much. No one had wanted to take the responsibility of forcing her back into a saddle.

No one, that is, except Garrett Coltrane.

Katy's mouth tightened ominously, and she turned away from the kitchen window. She had surrendered on every front to that man. Damned if she would let him win in this arena, too.

But she knew, even as she swore to fight him, that it was going to be a difficult, never ending battle. Garrett would be steady and insistent and relentless.

Katy looked around herself, feeling trapped inside the big, beautifully furnished house. Garrett would be coming for her soon, urging her to go down to the stable and look at Shadow Silk. Katy decided she needed some breathing time. She picked up the keys to the Mercedes, grabbed her purse and went outside to where the car was parked in the driveway.

Garrett came out of the stable when he heard the car's engine being switched on.

"Katy!"

Resentfully she rolled down the window and waited as he strode briskly toward her. When he reached the vehicle, he shoved the Stetson back on his head, planted both hands on the roof and leaned down to talk to her.

"Just where in hell do you think you're going?" he asked softly.

"Shopping."

"We'll do the grocery shopping later. It can wait."

"I'm sure you'll be much too busy getting your new mare settled in," Katy told him. "So I'll go by myself." She put the car in gear and slammed her foot down on the gas pedal.

"Now, Katy, you listen to me. You're acting like a child." The Mercedes leaped forward, and Garrett hastily stepped back out of the way.

Katy glanced back only once in the rearview mirror as she raced down the tree-lined driveway. Garrett stood with his feet apart, his big hands on his hips, his expression grim as she drove out of sight.

Garrett watched until the Mercedes vanished, and then he walked slowly back toward the stable. He had been through a lot since his wedding day; he had learned a great deal about his surprisingly unpredictable wife. But he had never seen her in this mood.

"She'll calm down," he informed Shadow Silk a few minutes later. "Just give her a little time. She's a bit high-strung these days, but she'll settle."

Shadow Silk nickered politely and ambled over to investigate her new feeding arrangements.

By five o'clock that evening Garrett was wondering seriously about his own feeding arrangements. Katy had not returned from town, and he was due to leave for the cattlemen's meeting in another hour. He had assumed Katy would cook an early dinner. When she didn't show up by five-thirty, he opened the refrigerator and morosely examined the contents.

At five forty-five, Garret finally admitted to himself that he was worried. Regardless of her mood, Katy should have been home by now. For the first time he faced the fact that she might not be returning.

She couldn't do that to him. She wouldn't do that to him. She loved him.

But she hadn't said that since the wedding night. Garrett realized he was pacing the large kitchen, his hands flexing in restless movements the way they used to back in the days when he was sitting in a rodeo arena chute, waiting to explode through the gate on the back of a Brahma bull.

It had been a long time since he had felt that same mixture of tension and adrenaline. It was an unpleasant sensation at best, and this time around it was worse than in the old days because it was laced with raw fear.

The sound of the Mercedes in the driveway had an instant effect on the fear. It was converted almost magically into a blazing fury. Vaguely Garrett realized it was the first time that he had ever completely lost his temper with Katy. He launched himself toward the door and flung it open just as Katy came slowly, warily, up the steps. She was carrying a sack of groceries. She stopped short when she saw the look on his face.

"Hello, Garrett." Her voice was very soft. She didn't move.

"Just where in hell have you been?" The words were much too low and dangerous. Garrett knew it, but he couldn't do anything about it. He was feeling dangerous. In fact, he'd never felt quite like this in his whole life.

"I told you, I went shopping." She took a cautious step forward and stopped again when he showed no signs of moving. "Groceries." She indicated the sack in her arms.

Garrett's eyes flicked to the sack. He saw the way she was clutching it as though it were a shield. "You've been gone for hours."

"Sorry. Was I supposed to sign out when I left? Am I under a curfew?"

"Katy, don't push your luck. I've got almost nothing left in the way of patience. What you did this afternoon was silly, emotional and infantile. Did it occur to you I might be worried?"

"No." She risked another step and stopped again. "I figured you'd be too busy with your new horse."

"The mare belongs to you, Katy," he said through his teeth. "She's all yours, whether or not you ever put a saddle on her."

"I don't want her."

"That's too bad, because you've got her." Garrett stepped back, allowing Katy to cross the threshold. She did so slowly, reluctantly, and her obvious hesitation fanned the fires of his anger. "Katy, don't ever pull a stunt like this again."

Something flickered in her eyes, a combination of resentment and anguish. "Don't give me orders, Garrett. I've had it. You've won every battle since the day we were married, and I'm tired of being the loser, do you hear me?"

He stared at her. Was that really the way she saw things, he wondered. "Is that what our honeymoon has been to you? A series of battles?"

Her mouth tightened and her eyes slid away from his. She started toward the kitchen. "At times it seemed like that. I'm sick of it, Garrett. What you did this afternoon was the last straw."

He was outraged. He was also getting scared again. He handled his fear the way he always had, by fighting back. "The last straw?" He loomed in the kitchen door behind her. "I buy you the most beautiful little mare in the whole world and you tell me it's the last straw?"

Katy slammed the sack of groceries down onto the tiled counter and spun around. Her face was tight with emotion. "Why do you keep pushing me? I've given it to you all the way down the line. How much more do you want from me, dammit?"

The expression in her eyes pushed him over the edge. "Everything," he exploded. "I want everything."

"What gives you that right?"

"You're my wife, that's what gives me the right. Whether you'll admit it or not, you love me. One of these days you'll say it again, just the way you said it on our wedding night."

"And have you throw the words back in my face the way you did then?" she raged.

"I'd never do that. I didn't do it then and I won't do it this time, either. If you're really convinced that I threw your words of love back in your face, you have no one to blame but yourself. It was your damned female temper that made you see things that way. You went off the deep end because your wedding night didn't quite fit the rosy fantasy you had imagined ahead of time."

"Is that right?" she shot back. "Well, I've learned a few things on this honeymoon, thanks to you. But look who's playing around with rosy little fantasies now. Why do you want me to tell you I love you? What difference does it make to you? You don't even believe in love."

He took a step forward and halted, not trusting himself to touch her. "Has it ever occurred to you that you're not the only one who's learned a few things during the course of this crazy honeymoon?" he shouted.

Katy's eyes widened. "No."

"*No?*" He was enraged now. "No? You don't think I'm capable of learning? You think you've got a monopoly?"

Katy chewed on her lower lip. "Garrett, calm down. Take it easy."

"Don't talk to me as if I were a horse. I'm your husband."

"Yes, I know," she said very softly. "You're stubborn, arrogant, proud as the devil and equally infuriating on occasion, but for better or worse, you are my husband."

He couldn't figure out what she was thinking, but Garrett sensed the change in the atmosphere. "Katy, listen to me—" he began, only to be interrupted.

"No, you listen to me. I'm tired of losing battles."

"We're not fighting a war," he protested, suddenly anxious to get her off that subject. It was too close to the truth.

"That's a matter of opinion." She put her hands on either side of herself, gripping the edge of the counter behind her. Garrett realized she was bracing herself for something. "You said you never threw my words of love back in my face."

"That's the truth, Katy."

"You claim you've learned a few things during the past few days."

"I'd have to have been blind, deaf and dumb not to have learned a few things," he muttered.

She took a deep breath. "All right, let's find out just how much you have learned. What happens now if I tell you I love you?"

"That's easy," Garrett said without stopping to think. "I say it back."

Katy's mouth fell open in amazement. Neither she nor Garrett moved.

"Garrett, I love you," Katy finally whispered.

It was Garrett's turn to take a deep breath. "I know. I love you, too."

He held open his arms and she rushed into them, stumbling a little as her weak ankle gave way slightly. But he caught her safely in his arms and folded her close.

"I love you, Katy. I love you, I love you, I love you." Now that he had learned how to say it, he couldn't seem to stop.

She clung to him, her own words of love spilling from her lips. For a timeless moment they stood locked in each other's arms and let the wonder of what was happening envelop them. Garrett felt a deep sense of peace and an equally joyous sense of release. It was as if his need to love Katy had suddenly been set free to be acknowledged and indulged to the hilt. He felt drunk with reaction.

It was Katy who abruptly broke the embrace. "What about your meeting?" she asked shakily. She glanced at the kitchen clock. "You're going to be late."

"Who cares?" Garrett started to pull her back into his arms.

Katy laughed softly. "Don't be silly. You have to go and you'd better be on your way. We'll have all night to talk."

"Talking isn't what I plan to be doing tonight." He nibbled her ear.

"Too bad. You were just getting good at it, too."

"Don't tease the lion. He's had a rough afternoon."

"Pity the poor lion," Katy whispered, spearing her fingers lovingly through his hair.

"Oh, God, Katy, I love you so. I should have realized days ago exactly what I was feeling. I should have known—"

She shook her head, cutting off his awkward confession. "It's been a very educational honeymoon."

"It's not over yet," he reminded her.

"True. But we're going to have to take a short intermission while you attend that cattlemen's meeting."

"Katy, I don't want to leave you now."

It took her another ten minutes to get him out of the house. As she stood in the doorway and waved, Katy nearly laughed aloud with happiness. She didn't need Garrett's assurances to know that he would be back the instant the meeting was over. They would have the rest of the night to practice telling each other of their love.

Katy closed the door at last, almost giddy with relief and wonder. Garrett loved her. He had admitted it. Together they had battled their way through to the point where she had naively assumed they had started on their wedding day.

The good things in life sometimes take a while to gel, Katy decided as she wandered back into the kitchen and began unpacking groceries. The good things took a little extra work.

She knew what it was like to work at something that was important to her. She had learned those skills years ago when she had trained horses and herself for the show ring.

That thought brought Shadow Silk to mind. For the first time Katy allowed herself to think about Garrett's intentions. He had meant well, she knew. He had wanted to give her back something that had once been very important to her, something that he could share with her.

It was impossible to hold his intentions against him. Katy thought about that while she ate a leisurely meal of cold leftovers. The man was heavy-handed at times, straightforward and determined, even ruthless on occasion, but now that she had calmed down, she couldn't help but be touched by his goal.

Half an hour later, Katy let her dishes go into the sink with a clatter. Then she walked out to the hall closet and grabbed a windbreaker to put on over her jeans and long-sleeved pullover.

There was no reason not to go down to the stable and take a look at Shadow Silk, Katy told herself. She might have no intention of ever riding the mare, but she still loved horses, and Garrett had said that Shadow Silk was now hers.

A few minutes later Katy opened the stable door to find Shadow Silk safely ensconced in her new stall, knee-deep in golden straw.

It was Red Dazzle who was missing.

# 11

Katy hoped desperately that Red Dazzle had simply found his way out of the back of his closed stall into the paddock, but even as she hurried outside to double-check, something told her she was wasting her time. There was no hulking four-legged shape dozing peacefully in the cold moonlight. The gelding was gone.

As Katy went back inside the stable to check the lock on the stall door, she told herself firmly to calm down. Red Dazzle was an energy-conserving creature. He wouldn't have wandered far. There was no storm to spook him tonight.

A soft, inquisitive whicker announced Shadow Silk's interest in the unexpected activity. A beautifully shaped equine head appeared over the stall door. Katy held out her hand and let the mare nuzzle her palm.

"What's going on around here, Silk? What have you done with your stablemate?" Katy frowned as she fingered the closure on Red Dazzle's stall. "I know he's not the most handsome male in the world. Not particularly refined or well-bred. Definitely a working-class background and proud of it. But he's got heart, you know? And guts. Actually, he's got quite a few things in common with his owner." Katy thought about that for a moment and then added with a fleeting grin, "There is one major difference, of course. Garrett is no gelding."

Shadow Silk snorted in a ladylike fashion.

Katy gave up on the stall door. It wasn't going to tell her whether the closure had been opened manually or by a particularly clever equine mouth. Then she remembered the alarm system.

"It should have gone off, regardless of how the stall door got opened," Katy muttered to Shadow Silk. Anxiously she made her way into the tack room where the alarm system wiring had been installed.

The instant she opened the door and turned on the light, Katy saw the open cover of the control panel box. Someone had switched off the system.

Real anxiety set in now. Red Dazzle wasn't simply wandering around loose somewhere nearby. Someone had deliberately taken him out of his stall.

For the second time?

Katy couldn't imagine why anyone would be playing games with an aging quarter horse, but she didn't spend any more time speculating on the matter. She left the stable and started quickly up the hill toward the Brackens' cottage.

The night air was chilly, but the moonlight provided enough illumination to see the path that led toward the small house. Lamplight glowed through the windows. Nadine hadn't yet lowered the shades against the night.

Breathing quickly from the exertion of her rapid walk up the hill, Katy pounded sharply on the front door of the cottage. When there was no immediate answer, she tried again.

"Emmett? Nadine? It's Katy. Something's happened to Red Dazzle. You've got to help me find him."

Silence was the only answer. Katy stepped back, glancing toward the side of the house. Emmett's old pickup truck was parked there in the shadows. The Brackens had to be home.

Katy tried pounding on the door once more and when that proved useless, she stepped off the front step and went around to the living room window. Feeling as if she was doing something slightly illegal, she peered through the uncovered window.

Emmett Bracken was sprawled on the sofa in front of the fireplace, obviously asleep. A half-empty bottle of whiskey sat on the floor beside him. Emmett had gotten an early start on his evening drinking. Katy frowned to herself as she scanned the room. Everything was as she remembered it from her one visit the afternoon they had tested the new alarm system. There was the pair of old, expensive silver candlesticks on the mantle. Nadine had proudly told Katy they had been a gift from the Atwoods. They framed the old cigar box that sat in the middle of the wooden shelf.

The lid of the box was open.

Memory returned in a rush. Emmett had told Katy he kept a gun in that box. But the colorful box was empty now. Katy wondered if Nadine removed the weapon as a precaution when Emmett got drunk.

Disgusted, Katy turned away. She wasn't going to get any help from that source. Then she started worrying about what had happened to Nadine. Perhaps Emmett had gone into a drunken rage and frightened his wife into leaving for a while.

But the real question was how that scenario fitted in with the missing gelding. A prickle of apprehension went through Katy. The fact that Nadine Bracken and Red Dazzle were both missing began to seem like too much of a coincidence.

Katy stood in front of the cottage and used the vantage point to survey the moonlit stables below. Nothing moved in the shadows. Slowly she made her way around the house, peering into the darkness and wishing badly that she had a flashlight.

It wasn't until Katy reached the back of the cottage that she saw the moving figures silhouetted against the night sky. A horse was being led along the top of the cliffs. It had to be Red Dazzle.

Even as Katy watched in astonishment, horse and human dipped momentarily from sight behind a large outcropping.

"Oh, my God." Katy broke into a ragged, unsteady run. Every step sent a jolt of pain up through her weak ankle.

It had to be Nadine Bracken leading Garrett's horse along the cliffs, but it made no sense. Katy couldn't begin to imagine what Nadine wanted with Red Dazzle. Not being able to guess only made the situation more nerve-racking, however. Whatever Nadine was up to, Katy knew in her bones it was nothing good.

Memories of Nadine's dour, unhappy attitude flooded Katy's brain as she struggled to move as quickly as possible over the uneven ground. There was an old, twisted bitterness in Nadine. The woman felt she had been dealt a raw deal by fate. She saw her whole life as having been ruined when Silas Atwood's son died in that freak climbing accident.

For the first time Katy began to wonder just how warped Nadine Bracken's emotions really were.

The roar of the ocean on the beach below the cliffs concealed any sound Red Dazzle's hooves might have made. Katy anxiously scanned the moonlit shadows ahead, trying to catch fleeting glimpses of her quarry.

Fortunately, Red Dazzle was never in a hurry to get anywhere, and he seemed to have no inclination to speed up for the sake of the stranger who was tugging on the halter lead. Katy prayed the gelding would continue his slow, stubborn ways. She was having trouble catching up with the horse as it was. Her ankle was getting worse by the minute.

Still, she was closing the gap, and Katy was on the point of calling out to Nadine when intuition suddenly warned her just where the older woman was taking Red Dazzle.

Real fear crawled down Katy's spine as she finally began to understand where the horse was being led. Nadine was taking him to the same point on the cliffs where the Atwood heir had died years before.

Katy gasped and bit back what would surely have been a useless yell. Instead she concentrated on using all her energy to catch up with Nadine.

Katy was panting heavily by the time she came around the last clump of trees that lay between her and Nadine's goal. She stumbled in the sand and grabbed for the side of a boulder to steady herself. Nadine still hadn't heard her. The older woman was wholly intent on what she was doing. Katy stared in horror, trying to see clearly in the pale light.

Nadine had come to a halt at the top of the cliffs. She had positioned the gelding between herself and the sheer rock wall that fell to the beach. Then she took something out of her coat pocket and put it down on a nearby rock. She was still holding on to the halter lead. For the first time Katy saw clearly what the other woman was holding in her left hand. It was a pitch-fork.

"Go on, get back," Nadine hissed to a disinterested Red Dazzle. "Get back, I say." She jabbed at the horse with a pitch fork.

Red Dazzle snorted as the wicked weapon came toward him. For the first time he began to show some interest in his precarious situation. He backed away from the fork, flinging his head up in irritation. Nadine lifted her arm and started to make another pass with the pitchfork.

"Nadine! Stop it! *Stop it!*" Katy threw herself forward, feeling her ankle give way completely. She was flung awkwardly down onto the sand.

"What are you doing here?" Nadine demanded as she whirled to confront Katy. "You're not supposed to be here. Get out of here. I won't let you stop me."

Katy clambered unsteadily to her feet. There were still several yards between her and Nadine. She had to move carefully. Nadine could use the pitchfork on Red Dazzle long before Katy could get to her.

"What's going on here?" Katy asked. "What do you think you're doing?"

"I'm going to punish him," Nadine explained. She still held Red Dazzle's lead. The horse was beginning to move restlessly on the end of the rein.

"Punish the horse? Nadine, that's ridiculous. Why would you want to hurt Red Dazzle?" Katy tried to keep her voice calm and reasonable. Slowly she edged forward, ignoring the pain in her ankle.

"Stay back," Nadine warned. She waved the pitch-fork at Katy. "Don't come near me."

Katy halted. "Just tell me what you have against the gelding."

"It's not the horse," Nadine shouted, clearly goaded by Katy's denseness. "It's *him*."

"Who?"

"Your husband. The new owner." Nadine was breathing heavily. She kept the fork aimed at Katy. "It's your husband who has to be punished. He had no right, don't you see? No right to buy this place. This was Atwood land. As far as the eye can see, it was Atwood property. And it should have stayed that way. Don't you understand? My girl should have been an Atwood. This land should have become ours. Garrett Coltrane has no right here. No right at all. I'm an old woman and he's a strong man in his prime. There's not much I can do to Coltrane himself, but I can destroy something he loves. I can destroy this horse. Coltrane needs to be punished!"

"Nadine, it was Atwood's decision to sell the property. Garrett just happens to be the man who came along and bought it. He had nothing to do with Atwood's original decision. Nothing to do with what happened all those years ago when Atwood's son fell and broke his neck."

"Coltrane shouldn't be here!" Nadine shouted hoarsely. "He has no right to be here."

"Nadine, listen to me . . ."

Nadine ignored her. "I thought at first it might be you I should destroy. I thought about that a lot. A man in love would be crushed to lose his new young wife, I told myself. Then I saw right away how it was between you and Coltrane. You two weren't even sleeping together. Some honeymoon, I said to myself. There's something wrong here. Coltrane doesn't love her. I overheard that argument you two had the day Royce Hutton came over here, you know. I heard you say that Coltrane had married you because of your social connections. There was no love lost between the two of you, was there?"

Katy felt a wave of panic. She tried edging a few steps closer. Nadine didn't seem to notice. The woman was too caught up in her strange, convoluted fantasy world. "Nadine, put down the pitchfork and let me talk to you. Let me explain things to you."

The response was another menacing movement of the pitchfork. Nadine must have yanked on Red Dazzle's lead at the same time, because the horse stamped one foot and tossed his head. His ears flickered warningly. His rear hooves were getting dangerously close to the cliff edge.

"You don't have to explain anything to me," Nadine said. "I saw how it was between the two of you and then I decided I could punish Coltrane by making him realize he'd married a woman he not only couldn't love, but one he couldn't trust. I could convince him to divorce you. The new family he wanted to start here on Atwood land would be destroyed before it even began. I was sure he'd think you'd let Red Dazzle out of his stall the night the two of you went to Hutton's party. If the horse got himself hurt or killed, Coltrane would be furious with you. He'd hate you. I had a plan, you see. I was going to start doing all sorts of things to make him wonder about you. I wanted to put doubts in his mind, make him worry and sweat until he finally came to the conclusion he had to divorce you."

"But your plan never got off the ground because Garrett never believed I was the one who had let Red Dazzle out of his stall."

"After that things seemed to get better instead of worse between the two of you. You even started using the same bed. You got smart, didn't you? It was obvious you'd decided to seduce him, and like any man he was willing to take advantage of the situation. But I can still punish him. I can still turn him against you. Just because he's sleeping with you doesn't mean he can't be made to see things the way I want him to see them. Coltrane cares about this horse, you know. He has a real sentimental attachment to this old gelding. And when Coltrane finds him dead at the bottom of this cliff he's going to have to wonder if you were responsible."

"Why would he think that? He loves me, Nadine."

Nadine's face twisted in a dark scowl. "Loves you? That's a laugh. You and him had another big fight today, didn't you? You were mad as hell when you found out he'd bought that fancy little mare for you. When he finds Red Dazzle dead, Coltrane is going to think you killed his horse to get even with him for trying to make you ride again."

Katy went cold. "Garrett's not that stupid. He knows I'd never do anything like that."

"We'll see." Nadine lifted her chin with arrogant fury. "We'll just see what happens. I've got this all planned out. I even got Emmett started early on his whiskey tonight just so's he'd be out of the way. He stopped me last time, you know. The old fool. All his drinking has made him softheaded. He doesn't understand this is the only way."

Katy sucked in her breath. "The night the alarm went off in the stables? That was you?"

"Coltrane was out of town. I was going to take the gelding that night and force him off this cliff. Earlier I'd made Emmett show me how to work the alarm system. But Emmett followed me and stopped me that night. Then he accidentally set off the system himself. He was half drunk, as usual. He made me go back to the house just as you arrived. But I waited for another chance, and tonight I've got it. Coltrane is gone again and this time when he gets back, his favorite horse will be dead and you'll be the one he blames. You'll see."

"I'll tell him you did it," Katy cried.

"It'll be your word against mine, won't it? And he knows you were angry with him. You're the only one with a reason to want to hurt him. He knows you've got a temper and that you're high-strung."

"I am not temperamental and high-strung!" Katy shouted, beginning to feel both.

"He told Emmett you were," Nadine retorted triumphantly.

Katy abandoned that angle of attack. She went back to edging cautiously closer. "Nadine, stop this foolishness. Put down the pitchfork and give me Red's lead. I'll take him back to his stall where he belongs."

"No!" Nadine whirled around to confront Red Dazzle with the pitchfork. She jabbed fiercely at the horse. This time the tines of the fork scraped the chestnut colt.

Red Dazzle danced backward, his front hooves leaving the ground. He screamed his fear and rage.

Katy realized there was only a foot or two between Red's hind legs and the edge of the cliff. "Red," she called frantically and then she tried the low, sharp whistle Garrett had used the night they had found Red in the storm. The gelding's ears pricked forward in response, and he voiced his disapproval of the entire situation. He moved about in agitation.

"Go on, you stupid horse." Nadine dropped the lead and hefted the pitchfork with both hands.

Nadine couldn't jab at the horse and defend herself from Katy at the same time. Katy used the few seconds of advantage to lunge at the woman.

In the last instant, Nadine realized she was being attacked. She swung around, bringing the pitchfork through the air in a lethal arc. Katy sprawled flat to avoid the tines of the fork. Her hand groped for and found Nadine's ankle. She yanked hard.

Nadine screamed as she tumbled to the ground and began to thrash around. Katy gasped for air as she struggled to her feet. The surge of adrenaline in her bloodstream made it possible to temporarily ignore the agony in her ankle. Her toe struck the handle of the pitchfork and she leaned down to pick it up. She hurled it over the edge of the cliff.

Red Dazzle whinnied nervously and pranced as Katy started toward him.

"Hey, take it easy," Katy murmured, reaching for the trailing rein. "Take it easy, Red. It's just me. I know you've had a hell of a night, but it's all over now. We're going to take you back to your stall and tuck you in. This will all seem like a bad dream in the morning."

She kept up the low, soothing patter as she gently urged the horse away from the edge of the cliffs. Red Dazzle snorted and made low, irritating woofling noises, but he came forward obediently when Katy tugged the rein.

Behind her, Katy heard Nadine lumbering painfully to her feet, but she didn't turn around. She had her hands full with Red Dazzle at the moment and besides, the woman was now unarmed.

"I won't let you stop me," Nadine said fiercely. "Do you hear me? I won't let you stop me."

The new hysteria in the woman's voice finally caught Katy's attention. She glanced back over her shoulder in time to see Nadine reach for the small dark object she had taken out of her pocket earlier and placed on the boulder.

Belatedly an image of the empty cigar box on the Bracken mantle went through Katy's head. The gun Emmett kept there was gone. Katy had a sudden premonition about where it was now.

"I didn't want to use this," Nadine sobbed as she scrabbled about for the gun. "I didn't want to do it this way, but you're forcing me . . ."

Katy waited no longer. There was no way she could reach the gun ahead of Nadine, not with her weak, throbbing ankle. There was only one hope for both herself and Red Dazzle.

"Okay, Red," Katy said between her teeth as she used her good right leg to hop up onto a nearby rock, "dazzle me." Holding on to the long lead, Katy grabbed a fistful of mane and flung herself onto Red Dazzle's back.

It wasn't the most graceful of mountings, but Red Dazzle was apparently too surprised to complain.

"Let's get out of here." Katy leaned forward and dug her heels into Red's sides. She hung on for dear life because she had seen Red in action years ago. When they finally did move, good rodeo horses were like good sports cars. Very fast and very quick.

And then Red Dazzle showed Katy just what had made him one of the best quarter horses on the pro rodeo circuit. He went from a standing start to full gallop in less time than it took to blink an eye. Katy clung to the horse with both arms and tightened her thighs. The night wind whipped Red's mane into her face and tangled her own hair.

Katy heard the crack of sound behind her and knew Nadine had used the gun. But since Red didn't slow and Katy felt nothing, she assumed they were both all right. A few more seconds would take them well out of range.

The Mercedes headlights coming up the long driveway announced Garrett's return just as Red Dazzle came pounding around the corner of the big house. Katy tugged on the flying mane and the leading rein she still held in one hand.

"Whoa, Red," she murmured. "We're okay now. Take it easy."

The gelding responded almost too quickly. Sudden stops were his specialty. Katy nearly went flying from his back as he plowed to a halt almost directly in front of the Mercedes. She managed to cling to her perch, however, as Garrett slammed open the door of the car. He stood staring at horse and rider for an astounded second, and then he strode quickly forward to grab Red Dazzle's halter. The gelding blew heavily and dropped almost instantly back into his normal, relaxed state. Only his still-heaving sides gave evidence of his recent exertion.

"What the hell is going on here?" Garrett looked up at Katy.

"It's Nadine. She tried to kill Red Dazzle by forcing him over a cliff."

"She *what*?"

"Garrett, she's got a gun. The woman is insane."

"Where is she?" Garrett demanded.

"The last I saw of her, she was back on the cliffs with the gun. Red got both of us out of there just in time."

"Are you all right?"

Katy nodded breathlessly. "I'm fine. I'm worried about Red, though. He probably hasn't had that much exercise in ages."

"Red's okay," Garrett said with an absentminded slap on the chestnut's neck. "I keep him in good shape. Leave him here and get into the house. Lock the door and call the cops."

"Where are you going?" Katy asked anxiously.

"I'm going to find Nadine and put a stop to this nonsense."

"Garrett, I don't think you should go out on the cliffs. Nadine is crazy and she's got Emmett's gun."

"Just get into the house and call the cops." Garrett reached up and hauled her down from Red's back. When she stumbled against him and clutched him for support, he groaned. "What have you done to your ankle?"

"It's all right—really it is."

That wasn't exactly true, but there was no point going into specifics. The ankle hurt badly, but Katy knew perfectly well that she wasn't going to die from the injury. A quick look into her husband's face told her she wasn't going to succeed in stopping him from going after Nadine, either.

"Just promise me you'll be careful, Garrett."

"I'll be careful." He opened the front door of the house and thrust her into the safety of the hallway.

Katy hobbled painfully toward the telephone.

Garrett looped Red Dazzle's lead rein around a convenient bush and then went to look for Nadine Bracken. He didn't have to search very hard to find the defeated woman. As he neared the cliffs the sound of racking sobs guided him to where she sat hunched on a boulder. Without a word he reached down and removed the gun from her hand.

"It wasn't right that everything should change the way it did," Nadine said sadly.

A LONG TIME LATER that night Katy lay back against the pillows of the bed and waited impatiently for Garrett to come out of the bathroom. Her ankle was carefully bound in an elastic bandage, and she knew from experience that it would recover in a day or two.

In the meantime, she and Garrett had a lot to talk about. Between answering the questions the police asked, dealing with a drunken Emmett Bracken and restoring Red Dazzle to the peace and tranquility of his stall, there had been very little time to talk. On top of everything else, Garrett had fussed endlessly about Katy's ankle, until she had finally convinced him she could take care of it as well as any doctor. Katy smiled at the memory of his scowling expression as he'd watched her wrap the bandage herself, and in that moment the bathroom door opened.

Garrett stood in the doorway, a towel draped around his lean waist. "Well, I'm glad someone is finding this evening amusing," he muttered as he switched off the light and came toward the bed. "Personally, I've about had it. Me and old Red are getting too old for this kind of excitement."

"Oh, I don't know about that," Katy said. "You and old Red both seemed to hold up pretty well under the circumstances."

Garrett tossed back the covers, dropped his towel and came down onto the bed beside Katy. He cradled her in his arms, his hand moving idly in her hair. In the shadows his eyes gleamed behind his lashes.

"You," he announced, "have been one surprise after another since our wedding day."

"Variety is the spice of life," she reminded him.

"Yeah? Well, I've had enough for a while. It's about time this marriage finally settled down and ran itself the way it's supposed to."

"How's that?"

Garrett chuckled and dropped a quick kiss on her parted lips. "Beats me. When I married you, I thought I knew how marriage between us would work. It would be pleasant, predictable and reliable. You'd be undemanding and easy to manage. You didn't seem to be the temperamental type. We'd have professional interests in common, and we both seemed to find each other attractive enough to share a bed."

"Hah. That's putting it mildly, and you know it. You know perfectly well that I found you more than just attractive enough to go to bed with. I was head over heels in love with you. On top of that, you were the sexiest man I had ever met. I couldn't wait to go to bed with you. In fact, we would have wound up in bed together a lot sooner than our wedding night if you had shown a little more interest in the matter."

"I was an idiot," Garrett freely admitted.

"True."

"You don't have to agree with everything I say."

"I'm practicing being undemanding and easy to manage. Agreeing with everything one's husband says is part of the process," Katy explained seriously.

Garrett gave her a small, affectionate shake. "Undemanding, easy-to-manage wives do not spend all their time finding ways to bait their husbands."

"Is that right? What do they spend their time doing?"

"I'll be happy to demonstrate," Garrett said, starting to roll Katy over onto her back.

"Wait! I've got some questions." Katy held him off, both her hands planted on his broad shoulders. "What about Emmett and Nadine?"

"What about them?" Garrett nuzzled the tip of his wife's nose. "As far as I'm concerned, we've got openings for a new handyman and a new housekeeper."

"You're going to let Emmett go?"

"He's got his pension from Atwood and he's got Social Security. He won't starve. If he wants to go on working, he can find a job somewhere else."

"And Nadine?"

"Something tells me Nadine is going to be taken care of by the state for the next few years."

"Garrett, maybe we should think about this," Katy began earnestly. "After all, they've both lived here for years and—"

Garrett put his hand over her mouth and smiled down into her wide, questioning eyes. "Honey, we gave the Brackens all the rope they wanted, and it was you who almost got hanged. You and Red Dazzle. I'm not about to invite trouble by giving them any second or third chances. I want them off this property and that's final. This particular subject is not open for discussion. You're a little too softhearted about some things."

Katy sighed, knowing she had lost this small battle and knowing, too, that Garrett was probably right. She would never feel easy with either Emmett or his crazy wife around. Katy put out the tip of her tongue and touched Garrett's palm. He laughed and removed his hand.

"No more arguments on that score?" he asked.

"No. I hate to admit it, but I think you're right."

Garrett grinned. "Words like that are music to a husband's ears. Now that we've settled that matter, there's another I think we might as well get out of the way."

"What's that?" Katy eyed him, torn between wariness and laughter.

"This business of your midnight riding habits."

"Oh, that."

"Yes, that." Garrett tightened his hold on her. "I don't suppose you know what a shock it was to see you come flying around the corner of the house the way you did tonight? At full gallop in the moonlight? With no saddle or bridle?"

"It was rather adventurous of me, wasn't it?"

"It took a dozen years off my life," Garrett declared. "But at least now I won't have to listen to any more excuses about how you can't or won't ride again."

Katy thought about that. "Uh, Garrett?"

"Forget it, Katy. You got back on a horse tonight and you didn't collapse in terror, so don't try telling me you can't handle riding."

"It was odd," Katy admitted, remembering the rush of sensation she had experienced on Red Dazzle. "I guess I just didn't have time to think. In any event, there wasn't much choice. It was either ride your horse or face Nadine's gun."

"Sometimes life makes things simple for us," Garrett said with deep satisfaction."

"How's that?"

Garrett smiled down at her as he gathered her close. "I love you," he said. "How much simpler can things get?"

"Sometimes," Katy whispered, "loving someone can be very complicated."

"Only for a woman who lets her imagination get carried away. Now hush, sweetheart, and let me show you just how simple life can be."

Katy smiled up at him as he slipped the nightgown off over her head. "I love you, Garrett."

"I love you, too." He bent his head to brush her mouth with his own.

Katy's fingers slid into his dark hair, and her body twisted sensually beneath his. "I know," she said, "But it's nice to hear the words."

# *Harlequin Temptation*

## COMING NEXT MONTH

**For the millions who can't read
Give the Gift of Literacy**

One out of five adults in North America
cannot read or write well enough
to fill out a job application
or understand the directions on a bottle of medicine.

**You can change all this by joining the fight
against illiteracy.**

For more information write to:
Contact, Box 81826, Lincoln, Neb. 68501
In the United States, call toll free: 1-800-228-8813

**The only degree you need
is a degree of caring**

LIT-A-1R